Slaying at the Saloon

NIGHTMARE ARIZONA
PARANORMAL COZY MYSTERIES

BETH DOLGNER

Slaying at the Saloon
Nightmare, Arizona Paranormal Cozy Mysteries, Book Three

Print ISBN-13: 978-1-958587-12-6

Slaying at the Saloon is a work of fiction. Names, characters, places, and incidents either are the products of the author's imagination or are used fictitiously. Any resemblance to actual persons, living or dead, businesses, companies, events, or locales is entirely coincidental.

Published by Redglare Press
Cover by Dark Mojo Designs
Print Formatting by The Madd Formatter

bethdolgner.com

CHAPTER ONE

"Please continue to hold. Your call is important to us. By our estimate, a customer service associate will be with you in approximately thirty-two minutes."

"You told me it was thirty-one minutes four minutes ago!" I shouted at the automated voice on the other end of the line.

"Olivia." Damien's voice was firm, frustrated. And the more I heard it, the more it annoyed me.

"This whole thing is stupid, anyway," I grumbled.

Damien sighed and flopped back against the love seat in my little apartment. "You have to update your car insurance, anyway, so it makes sense to use this as an exercise in controlling your conjuring skills."

"Maybe," I said through clenched teeth, "I should be wishing to get a real human being on the line so I can get this done. Instead, you want me to be *patient.*"

"Learning to control your emotions is a huge part of learning to control your abilities. If you can't even wait on hold without getting frustrated, then how are you going to react in a high-stress situation?" Damien had already shed his suit jacket, leaving him in his charcoal-gray pants and a black button-down shirt. As I glared at him, he began to roll his cuffs up, exposing his muscular forearms.

Too bad I can't get another look at those biceps.

I blushed at that thought, which at least helped distract me from the fact I had been on hold for twenty minutes already. I had put the cell phone on speaker, and tinny jazz music emanated from it, making my apartment feel more like an elevator.

"I like to think I do better in an emergency than I do when I'm waiting for customer service," I said defensively. In fact, when faced with a real do-or-die situation, I had a bad habit of freezing up. It was pretty much the opposite of letting my emotions get out of control; they would just shut down completely.

Damien leaned forward, resting his elbows on his knees. "Please stop that."

"Stop what?" When he raised an eyebrow at me and nodded in my direction, I paused, wondering what he could be talking about. Then I heard it. A rhythmic *tap-tap* barely audible over the music coming from the flip-phone Damien had loaned me. I was drumming my fingernails on the small Formica table that sat in front of my equally diminutive kitchenette. I slapped my palm flat on the table. "Sorry."

Damien absolutely believed I was some kind of supernatural being called a conjuror, a person who could want something so badly they actually made it happen. He thought it was how I had gotten a job at Nightmare Sanctuary Haunted House, even though there were no openings at the time. I didn't know how or why the index card advertising the job had shown up on Nightmare's local job board, nor did I know why it had been in the handwriting of Baxter Shackleford, who had gone missing six months before the notice appeared.

What I did know was that I was just an average, ordinary, nothing-special human.

Still, Damien insisted on giving me lessons to control my alleged abilities, because he was convinced I could be dangerous otherwise. I knew he was doing it partly out of fear about his own unexplored supernatural abilities, but I had agreed to play along.

Because, if there was any chance I *was* a conjuror, then maybe I could use those skills to find Baxter. As Damien's father and the owner of Nightmare Sanctuary, there were a lot of people who wanted to find him and bring him home safely.

I sighed. "Okay, if we're going to be sitting here for another half an hour or so, can you please run down to the vending machines and get me some chocolate chip cookies?" Without waiting for Damien to answer, I got up and grabbed my purse off my bed, then fished out three quarters.

Damien's mouth twisted into something that was half frown, half amused smile. "Will eating cookies help you control your emotions?"

"I think it's a theory worth testing."

Damien disappeared out my front door. I lived in an efficiency apartment in the rear corner of Cowboy's Corral Motor Lodge, and having the vending machines and an ice machine downstairs was handy. I counted out ten seconds, long enough for Damien to get down the steps that led to the ground floor, and let out a loud yell. I just needed to express my frustration in vocal form.

The on-hold music didn't care. It kept playing, like I wasn't fighting the urge to chuck the phone out the window.

When Damien got back, he handed me the cookies while peering at me with his green eyes. "The walls of this motel aren't that thick, you know. Shouting is not controlling your emotions."

In answer, I ripped open the package of cookies and shoved one into my mouth.

And, of course, that was the moment a voice on the

other end of the line said, "Hello, thank you for your patience. May I please have your name and policy number?"

"Offvaa Kinnduck," I said around a mouthful of cookie.

"Olivia Kendrick," Damien said, sitting down at the table with me. He picked up the plastic insurance card and read off my policy number.

Once the call was done, I looked at Damien with a smirk. "You've been teaching me to control my emotions, but the minute I let my emotions out, I got someone on the phone, thirty minutes before the automated system said I would."

Damien ran a hand through his wavy dark-blond hair. "That's the problem, Olivia. When you let your emotions go, you're unleashing your power. It served you well just now: you got someone on the line. You got what you wanted. But what if the thing you wanted was more sinister? What if, say, someone rear-ended your car, and you got so angry you shouted that you wished they had gotten hurt to learn a lesson? You might actually cause that person to have injuries."

I closed my eyes to prevent myself from rolling them and reminded myself that even though I didn't take this whole conjuring business seriously, Damien certainly did. "You're right," I said. I didn't even open my eyes as I grabbed another cookie. As far as I was concerned, getting the customer service rep on the line earlier than expected had just been a coincidence. To Damien, it was proof of my supernatural ability.

"It's not the lesson I was trying to teach you, but I think it was valuable nonetheless," Damien said. "And it's a good thing you wrapped up the call, because you need to get to the saloon."

I opened my eyes and glanced at the clock on the wall.

I was due to meet my Sanctuary friends and co-workers at Nightmare Saloon in just twenty minutes. "You sure you don't want to come with us?" I asked. I had been trying to convince Damien that if he was going to run Nightmare Sanctuary in his father's absence, then he needed to socialize with its employees.

"I know where I'm not wanted," Damien mumbled as he stood. "I'll see you tomorrow."

"You'll see me the day after tomorrow. Remember, I'm off on Tuesday nights, too." I paused, then said, "Thank you for the lesson."

"Of course." Damien didn't even say goodbye. He just let himself out, and I was suddenly alone.

I changed out of my shorts and T-shirt and into dark-blue jeans and a periwinkle blouse. I gave my shoulder-length auburn hair a quick fluff, touched up my makeup, and headed out.

It was early September, and it was already dark, but it was hot out, nonetheless. By the time I had made the walk from the motel to High Noon Boulevard, I was fanning myself with one hand.

Nightmare Saloon was on the town's tourist street, High Noon Boulevard. The historic Old West buildings along the street had been preserved, and the asphalt had been covered with dirt to make it look like an authentic street from the late eighteen hundreds. Covered wooden boardwalks ran down each side of the street, and during the day, tourists would huddle under their shade to watch gunfight reenactments and other costumed actors who portrayed the Wild West.

The saloon was as much a part of the show as the actors. The entrance had short swinging doors, making it look like something from a Western movie set. Inside, dark wood paneling and low lighting from dusty chandeliers really set the mood. Mondays were typically quiet in

Nightmare, since tourists mostly flocked to the former mining boomtown on weekends, but on this evening, I walked in to see nearly every seat was occupied.

I found my friends at two tables near the front, their chairs already turned to face the low stage, which was hidden by a thick red curtain trimmed in gold fringe. Thankfully, they had saved a seat for me, and I slid into it. "Wow, I didn't realize this musician was so popular!" I said in greeting.

"Allie was great the last time she played in Nightmare," responded Theo. He was looking particularly handsome this evening, even though he was only wearing jeans and a white T-shirt. His brown hair flowed down to his shoulders, and his brown eyes always had a mischievous look. Theo grabbed the pitcher of beer sitting on the table, filled an empty glass, and slid it toward me. "You look like you need this," he said, grinning. Even though he was a vampire, Theo had no fangs, so his teeth looked totally normal.

I thanked Theo and raised the glass toward him, then took a sip. Before I could swallow, though, the pitcher began to slide along the table by itself, and I gasped, then coughed. Malcolm gave me a thump on the back with a pale, bony hand.

While my other friends from the Sanctuary tended to dress normally when they left the year-round haunted house where most of them lived and worked, Malcolm was in his usual long black coat and top hat. His tall form and gaunt features made him stick out in a crowd, anyway, so I guessed he figured there was no point in changing his outfit.

"Sorry, Olivia." It was Justine, and the pitcher was just coming to a stop in front of her. "It's a bad habit." Justine, who managed the Sanctuary, had telekinetic abilities, and even though I knew that, I had never seen her move something with just her mind until that moment.

"It's a pretty cool trick," I told her with a playful wink, "but forewarn me next time!"

The overhead lights dimmed, and the footlights across the front of the stage began to glow more brightly. "Here we go!" Mori said excitedly. She turned to me, her burnt-orange eyes intense even in the low lighting. "You're going to love Allie's voice. And I'm not biased just because she's a vampire like me." Unlike Theo, Mori did have her fangs, and they gleamed as she smiled at me.

Just a week before, I had found out Allie Nunes was a singer who toured the country on what Theo referred to as "The Supernatural Circuit." He had explained Allie favored tour stops in towns with a lot of supernatural creatures, even though she was popular with humans, too. Since Allie was a vampire, it made sense many of her fans would be supernatural.

The red curtain rose slowly, and a spotlight illuminated the center of the stage, but there was no one standing there in front of the microphone. A few people at the table in front of ours gasped, and one woman cried out. I leaned forward, trying to figure out what they were seeing that I wasn't.

There was something on the floor of the stage, but I couldn't tell what it was since the heads and shoulders of the people in front of me were in the way. I half rose from my chair, and immediately wished I hadn't.

There was a woman dressed as a saloon girl sprawled on the stage, her open eyes staring blankly upward. A wooden stake was protruding from her chest.

CHAPTER TWO

I pressed a hand to my mouth and sat down stiffly. Around me, a wave of cries and shouts was spreading through the room as more and more people realized what they were seeing. There was a dead woman on the stage.

No, not a dead woman, I realized. *A murdered woman.*

See what I mean about me freezing during a crisis? If Damien were there, I probably would have said, "I told you so." I wasn't upset or crying or any of the many things going on around me. Instead, I was quietly seated in my chair, feeling slightly numb.

I turned to Theo, whose eyes were darting around wildly. His fingers, I noticed, were gripping the edge of the table so hard he was leaving fingernail marks in the wood. His obvious fear finally elicited a proper reaction from me. I grabbed his face with my hands. "Theo, is it her? Did someone kill Allie?"

Theo shook his head almost imperceptibly. I felt it under my hands more than I saw it. "No," he said quietly. "That's not her. But I think it was supposed to be."

"What do you mean?"

Malcolm leaned toward us. "He means the woman has a wooden stake through her heart. This looks like the work of a vampire slayer."

Oh, no wonder Theo looks terrified. I glanced at Mori and

saw that she, too, was keeping a wary eye on the people around us, though she seemed less upset than Theo. "A vampire slayer? What, did they stake the wrong person?" Even as I was asking, I remembered the dead woman was dressed as a saloon girl, meaning she was likely a server at the saloon.

"Maybe," Malcolm said. "It's also possible a slayer did it to scare Allie."

"Or one of us," Theo moaned.

Zach was one of the Sanctuary employees seated at the table next to ours. He leaped out of his chair and shot toward us. My hands were still on Theo's cheeks, and I finally dropped them into my lap as Zach leaned down and said to him, "You and Mori need to leave, now. Malcolm and I will get you back to the Sanctuary."

Theo nodded, but Mori said, "And what about Allie? We can't just leave her!"

"I'll stay," I said. "I'll go find her backstage."

"Me, too." Justine stood up, her long chestnut-brown hair swinging gracefully with the motion. "Be careful, all of you."

In a flash, Malcolm, Zach, and the others had escorted Theo and Mori out of the saloon. I said a silent prayer they would make it safely back to the Sanctuary even as Justine grasped my hand and pulled me up.

There was a door to the left of the stage that had an old-fashioned brass plaque on it reading *BACKSTAGE*. We had to elbow our way past the people who were crowding around the stage, even though someone was already lowering the curtain to block the view of the murdered woman. Once we went through the door, we found ourselves in a long, bright hallway that was lined with doors on the left-hand side. A door about halfway down stood open, and a man with small anxious-looking eyes behind wire-rimmed glasses was leaning out of the doorway, staring right at us.

"We're looking for Allie," Justine called to him. "We're from Nightmare Sanctuary."

The man's face relaxed a fraction, and he waved us forward. "Come on."

We hurried down the hall and into a small dressing room that looked like it had been in need of renovation for at least two decades. There was a beat-up white makeup table against the far wall, and the lighted mirror above it had several jagged cracks in the corners. A woman sat on a stool in front of the table, staring at herself while slowly twirling a lock of her long strawberry-blonde hair. Her eyebrows were drawn together over intense blue eyes.

"Oh!" I said. "She has a reflection."

The woman turned to me in surprise. "Of course I do. Who are you?"

"I'm Justine Abbott, and this is Olivia Kendrick," Justine answered for me. "We both work at Nightmare Sanctuary Haunted House. You're safe with us. Olivia is new to our world, so please forgive her."

Even amid the fear and confusion, I suddenly worried I had committed some kind of supernatural faux pas, but Allie looked at me kindly. "Don't believe everything you read in novels. We have reflections just like anybody else." She nodded toward the man, who was staring at the hallway behind us. "That's my manager, Jon. He's human."

"Me, too," I said, giving Jon a polite smile of human solidarity. He didn't seem to notice. Instead, he kept his gaze fixed on the doorway. I turned and shut the dressing room door, and Jon finally seemed to snap into the present moment. He tore his eyes away from the door and gave Justine and me a tentative nod.

"We're worried this might be the work of a slayer," Justine said, getting straight to business.

"Us, too," Allie agreed.

"If you're here to be bodyguards, though, I don't think it's necessary." Jon ran a shaking hand through his short brown hair. "We can fend for ourselves."

I wanted to argue that he looked like he might quail if someone so much as raised their voice to him, but Allie spoke up first. "Someone was just murdered, and it looks like a vampire execution. I'll take all the protection I can get, thank you."

For a brief moment, Jon looked annoyed, but he soon looked scared and anxious again.

"We can take you to the Sanctuary," I said. "It will be easy to guard you there."

Allie shook her head. "No. Not yet. If I run away, the police will think I'm fleeing the scene." Allie and Jon exchanged a brief but worried glance. "I have to stay here until the police say I can go."

"Then we'll stay with you," Justine said. There were a few folding chairs leaning against one wall, and she quickly set up two of them so we could sit. Jon, on the other hand, stood near the door, his eyes darting between it, Justine, and me. I wanted to tell him to calm down, but I figured we didn't know each other quite well enough for that yet.

"Do you know the woman?" I asked Allie.

"I don't know. Maybe. I left the dressing room and went through the door that leads to stage right. Frankie said to wait just inside the door, and to walk to center stage when the spotlight lit up. Except when the spotlight came on…"

"Did you hear anything while you were waiting there? Any muffled cries or sounds of a struggle?"

Jon made a noise that was part disgust and part laughter. "What are you, the town detective?"

"She's trying to help," Allie said. She looked surprised by Jon's response to my questions. "And no, I didn't hear anything. I don't know when that poor girl was murdered, but it didn't happen in the minute or so I was standing there waiting for my cue. I saw the ruffled black skirt and the red corset, and I saw that wooden stake. I didn't stop to look at her face before I ran back here. So, to answer your original question, I don't know who it is lying on that stage right now. I've talked to a number of the servers here this evening, but I don't know which one was killed."

"Who's Frankie?" Justine asked.

"The owner of the saloon," Jon said impatiently. He had pulled a key ring out of his pocket and was slowly sliding each key from one side to the other. His anxious behavior was keeping my own heart from getting back down to a normal pace, so I looked away.

"Yeah," Allie added, "he's our main contact here. We scheduled the show through him. The last time we were here… Oh, no! My guitar! It was leaning against the wall while I was waiting for the curtain to rise. Jon, can you please go get it?"

Jon turned his head in slow motion to stare at Allie. "Are you kidding me? There's a murderer out there, and you want me to go get your *guitar*? Are you trying to get me killed, too?"

Allie shook her head. "Never mind," she said quickly. "You're right. It was stupid of me to ask."

"I'll go get it," I said, rising. When Allie began to protest, I waved a hand. "The police station is right down the street, which means they're here already, and the killer is probably long gone. I won't be in any danger."

Jon took a long step back to keep his distance from me as I approached the door. Either that, or he was trying to get as far away from his imagined death as he could. I meant what I had said to Allie: I was absolutely convinced it was perfectly safe for me to leave the dressing room.

Still, to make her and Jon feel better, I opened the dressing room door and dashed out as quickly as I could so they wouldn't feel exposed. Farther down the hallway was a door with a police officer standing guard beside it. Knowing it must be the door that led to the stage, I headed toward it.

I went exactly two steps before the officer looked at me, crossed his arms, and said, "Of course it's you."

I tried to smile in a casual, "fancy meeting you here" sort of way, but I'm sure it was more of a grimace. "Officer Reyes," I said. "I just need to grab Allie's guitar for her. She said she leaned it against the wall just through that door."

"You know the singer?" Reyes's eyes narrowed suspiciously.

"She's the friend of a friend, and she's shaken up by what happened, so I said I'd keep her company."

"How do you always wind up in the middle of our murder investigations?"

I raised my hands defensively. "I just came to see the show tonight! I am not involved in your murder investigation whatsoever."

Reyes sighed. "Good. I hope it stays that way. I need to question Ms. Nunes, anyway. I'll grab her guitar and meet you both in the dressing room."

I thanked Reyes and hustled back to the dressing room, so I could let the others know the questioning was about to begin. Reyes soon joined us, and after he handed over Allie's guitar, he looked at me pointedly. "I need to talk to Ms. Nunes and her manager privately."

"We'll wait in the hallway," I said, already walking toward the door.

"Wait!" Allie rose from her stool, one arm held out

toward me. "I don't know… I'm not…" Her eyes flicked to Reyes nervously.

She's worried he might be the vampire slayer.

"I met Officer Reyes during a murder investigation about six weeks ago," I said in as reassuring a tone as I could muster.

"And then a couple weeks ago, during another murder investigation," mumbled Reyes.

I spared him a brief glare, then continued, "You're in safe hands."

That seemed to be good enough for Allie, whose stance relaxed slightly. As we walked out, Officer Reyes asked for their full names. "Alexandra Nunes and Jonathan Holcomb," Allie answered in a quavering voice.

I didn't hear any more, because two officers had just come through the stage door, and they ushered Justine and me out into the saloon, despite our protests that we were waiting for Allie. The lights had been turned up in the saloon, and the only people in there were employees and police. Justine sat down at the table nearest the backstage door, but I paced toward the front of the saloon, hoping to catch a bit of the fresh air coming through the front doors.

Another woman dressed as a saloon girl was standing next to a man wearing a plaid Western shirt and brown chaps over his jeans. "It's karma, if you ask me," the woman said, her tone biting. "She stole from Frankie, and now she's dead."

CHAPTER THREE

I slowed down to eavesdrop as clandestinely as I could, but the cowboy—whom I recognized as a bartender at the saloon—responded in such a low voice I couldn't hear him. When the two of them walked off, I was left to wonder what, exactly, the dead woman had stolen from the owner of Nightmare Saloon.

I was also left wondering if Frankie had killed her because of it. But, I told myself, surely no one would be dumb enough to commit murder at their own place of business. Or maybe it wasn't dumb, but absolutely brilliant because it would automatically make them seem like less of a suspect.

Then again, I remembered, it might have been a vampire slayer who did this, and the server I'd overheard was merely trying to make sense of a senseless murder.

"Not my business," I said quietly to myself. I was there to make sure Allie and Jon stayed safe, and that was it. There was no way I was going to wade into yet another murder investigation.

The night air felt good as it wafted over the top of the swinging doors, and I closed my eyes while I breathed it in. Of course, it was hard to truly enjoy the moment since there was a crowd of people huddled outside, all staring toward me. The police had cordoned off the saloon entrance, looping yellow tape around the posts that supported the roof of the boardwalk, but it looked like half of Nightmare was just beyond it, standing expectantly in the dirt-covered street.

"Olivia," Justine called.

I looked over to see her waving me toward the backstage door, where she was standing with Officer Reyes.

"Ms. Kendrick," Reyes said seriously, "I know I teased you about showing up at another murder investigation, but I'm giving you and your friend here a task. Ms. Nunes and Mr. Holcomb are not to leave town until we have solved this case. I'm counting on the two of you to keep a close watch on them."

I was too surprised to say much, but I agreed, and soon, Reyes stalked away from us. He hopped up onto the stage, lifted the edge of the curtain, and slipped under it without giving us any view of what was happening behind it.

"I think the safest place for them is the Sanctuary," Justine said. "We can protect them if this really is the work of a vampire slayer. Plus, if they're staying there, keeping an eye on them can be a team effort."

"I was thinking the same thing."

Allie was packing her guitar into its case when Justine and I got back to the dressing room. Justine immediately proposed her idea, adding, "There are windowless guest rooms for vampires, and our werewolf, Zach, does a security patrol. You'll be safe."

"I'd rather be on the road. I can't make money if I'm stuck here," Allie grumbled.

"It's a free place to stay, at least," I pointed out.

Allie sighed, and her shoulders slumped. "I'm sorry if I sound ungrateful. I'm just upset about this whole situation. And scared."

"We'll make the best of it," Jon said tightly, patting Allie's arm.

Since Allie and Jon were touring in a van, Justine and I helped them load up, found places to sit among the luggage and music gear, then gave Jon directions to the Sanctuary. Soon, the van crested the hill in the dirt lane that led to the former hospital building, and the headlights swept across the dirty gray stone facade.

Malcolm and Zach came outside as we were helping Allie and Jon unload their suitcases, and soon, we were all inside the tall, grand entryway of the Sanctuary. Zach handed the bag he was carrying to Justine. "You and Malcolm can get our guests settled in. There's a basement room ready for Allie. I need to talk to Olivia."

As soon as the others had disappeared down the East Wing hallway, Zach turned to me and said quietly, "Theo is really upset."

"Of course he is. There might be a vampire slayer in town."

Zach shook his head. "No, I mean he's really upset. He didn't speak the whole walk back here, and then he just disappeared. None of us knows where he went."

I bit my lip. Theo was usually easygoing, but I knew he could get riled up when the occasion called for it. Scared so badly that he would hide, though? That didn't seem like him. Rather, he had always struck me more as the type who would run toward danger without worrying about possible consequences. "There's at least one psychic here, right? Or maybe the witches can do some kind of finding spell," I suggested.

"It won't be necessary. He's in the cemetery vignette." It was Mori's voice, and I turned to see her standing a short distance away. Her black hair, which had been swept up into an elegant coiffure earlier, was slightly askew, and I thought I saw a damp streak running down the dark skin of one cheek.

I heard a whimper, and I looked down to see Mori's pet chupacabra, Felipe, crouched behind her legs. He had one clawed paw wrapped around her calf, and he was peeking up at Zach and me with wide, dark eyes.

"You're scared, too," I said. Even as I spoke, I crouched down and opened my arms to Felipe. He slowly crept toward me, then climbed into my arms. He was heavy, but I picked him up and scratched his gray, leathery head.

"Slayers are rare, Olivia," Mori said. "Even more rare than shapeshifters, and that's saying a lot. I've been undead for four hundred years, and I've never once encountered a slayer. So, yes, I'm scared."

Felipe nuzzled against my shoulder. "Have you considered the wooden stake was just a coincidence?" I asked gently.

Mori's shoulders twitched in a half-hearted shrug. "I suppose it could be, but it would be a big coincidence."

I heard footsteps and turned to see Damien coming toward us from the direction of his office. He stopped short and stared at me. "What's going on?"

"Allie and Jon can't leave town until the murder investigation is wrapped up, so Justine and I told them they can stay here." I could hear the edge to my voice, daring Damien to disagree with me.

Instead, he tilted his head. "Who? What murder?"

I rounded on Zach. "You didn't tell Damien yet?"

Zach, at least, looked slightly embarrassed as he said, "I was getting to that."

Damien's jaw clenched. "My office, right now." He glanced at Mori. "All of you."

We followed dutifully, like children who knew they were about to be scolded. Once we were inside the office, which really belonged to Damien's father, Mori and I settled onto the oxblood leather chairs that sat in front of the expansive desk. Zach stood just behind Mori's chair, and Felipe scrambled out of my arms so he could curl up on the threadbare rug.

Damien moved behind his desk but remained standing. "Tell me everything," he said.

Mori summed up our evening quickly, ending with her flight back to the Sanctuary with Theo, Malcolm, and Zach.

"Justine and I stayed to keep Allie safe, in case it really is a vampire slayer on the loose," I said. "When the police talked to her and her manager, Jon, they were told not to leave town until this is all wrapped up. So, we brought them back here so they can safely stay in one of the basement apartments."

Damien raised his face toward the ceiling, and I could see his jaw muscles clench again. He took several deep breaths, then said in a quiet, even tone, "Are you out of your mind?"

"We thought this would be the safest place for them," I said.

"Making it the most dangerous place for Mori and Theo, if there really is a slayer after this Allie woman. And"—Damien finally lowered his head, and he braced his hands on his desk so he could lean toward me—"it's entirely possible one of them is the actual murderer, making their stay here dangerous for every single one of us."

I slid forward in my chair and glared at Damien defiantly. "In that case, having them here is the best way to keep an eye on them."

There was the sound of quick, light footsteps in the hallway outside Damien's office, and I turned in time to see Justine appear in the doorway. "Damien, we need to—oh. You've already been briefed, I see."

Damien straightened up, and I caught just a hint of a green flash in his eyes. He could be added to the list of people at the Sanctuary who were upset by the events of the evening, right alongside Theo and Mori. And Felipe, for that matter. "I think this is a dangerous plan," he said.

Justine glanced at me, then back to Damien. "We'll all keep a close eye on Allie and Jon, and an even closer eye on the grounds. We'll form teams to help Zach with security. Please, Damien. She's a vampire. Where else can Allie be safe in this town?"

Damien's chest heaved, and I suddenly wondered if his reaction to Allie and Jon staying at the Sanctuary wasn't just concern for himself and his employees. His father had taught him to lock away his supernatural abilities the second he exhibited signs of them as a teenager. Damien didn't know what Baxter was, and that meant he didn't even know what he was, or what he might be capable of. Because he hadn't been allowed to embrace his supernatural abilities, Damien had always been the outsider at the Sanctuary. I knew that was partly by choice. While I had been made to feel welcome immediately, despite not being supernatural—whatever Damien might say to the contrary—Damien's resentment stood between him and every single person at the Sanctuary, including his own father. I didn't think Damien liked that Allie had been so quickly invited to stay despite the danger she brought with her. She seemed to fit in at the Sanctuary even more than Damien, who had grown up there.

"Fine," Damien said after a long, tense silence. "But if there is any sign of trouble, you two"—Damien pointed at Justine and me—"are responsible for getting our guests out of here."

"Agreed," Justine and I said in unison.

"I'm going to get them some fresh sheets and towels," Justine said.

"I'll help you," Zach said quickly. I couldn't blame him for wanting to get away from Damien as soon as possible.

Mori and I stood and turned to go, but before we could, Theo appeared in the doorway. He had a duffel bag in one hand.

"I'm not staying here with Allie," Theo said firmly, though he still looked terrified.

Damien stepped up next to me and gave me a sidelong glance. "Even more reason why she and her manager shouldn't be staying here."

"Theo," Mori said, stepping forward to grasp his hand, "I'm scared, too, but Allie will be safest here."

"Besides," I said, "as I told Mori a bit ago, it's entirely possible this murder has nothing to do with vampires. It was a human who was killed, so it probably wasn't a vampire slayer who did this."

"Right now, we have no way to be sure," Mori said uncertainly.

"Which means it could have been a slayer." Theo shook his head grimly. "And of everyone here at the Sanctuary, I'm the only one who knows what a vampire slayer is capable of."

CHAPTER FOUR

Mori gasped, and I saw her hand clamp even tighter around Theo's. "You never told me you'd met a slayer before." She sounded scared.

"Because I don't like to talk about it." Theo looked at Damien. "Baxter knows. I told him what happened when I first came here, looking for a safe haven, but I've never told the story to another soul."

"If you're willing," Damien said, "will you please tell us about your experience? It could be useful for us if this is, in fact, a slayer we're dealing with."

Theo swallowed hard, then gave a curt nod. He dropped Mori's hand, shut the office door, and began to pace in front of the stone fireplace at one side of the office. "You all know I was a pirate in the seventeen hundreds. I spent most of my time with a ship called *The Tempest*, which sailed the Caribbean. Six of us on the crew were vampires, and we would feed—" Theo cut off abruptly and glanced at me, then cleared his throat. "Well, no need to go into details about that. Suffice to say I was a very different kind of vampire back then. Anyway, we had a daytime crew of humans, and then the six of us who were on the night crew.

"We anchored off Port Royal one night to make a supply run. We took a rowboat to shore, and while we were walking down an alley toward a storehouse, one of our men cried out. We all watched as he turned to dust. At first, we didn't know how it had happened; we just knew he was dead."

Mori dropped into her chair. "How awful. What did you do?"

"We ran, of course." Theo blew out a breath. "I heard something whistle past me, and I knew it was an arrow. The wooden shaft of the arrow would act like a wooden stake: if it went through my heart, I would be dust, too. Unfortunately, we were sitting ducks in that alley. It dead-ended at the storehouse, and by the time we reached the door, another one of our men was gone."

The look of anguish on Theo's face was so intense I had to turn my head away. Even now, more than two hundred years after the incident, I could see how much pain the memory still caused him.

"We broke the lock on the storehouse door and ran inside," Theo continued. "There was a window at the back, and I headed right for it. As I was crawling out ahead of the first mate, I felt a spray of dust against my back and knew there were only three of us remaining. We split up, agreeing we would each find a safe place to hide until the next night, when we would meet at the rowboat. I made it to the edge of town and hid in a barn loft.

"The next night, I awoke at sunset and made my way back to the shoreline where we had left our boat. It was still there, but my two remaining shipmates didn't come. I waited for hours, then finally gave up and decided to row back by myself. I could, at least, send the human crew to search for the others."

Theo stopped again and rubbed a hand along the back of his neck. "He was waiting for me in the rowboat, lying down so I wouldn't see him until I was practically on top of him."

"The slayer?" I asked breathlessly.

Theo nodded. "I thought that was it for me, and I felt this strange peace wash over me. I was about to die, and I was okay with it. But he didn't stake me. Instead, he opened a small box that had an incredibly bright light inside it. It must have been magical, because it was like he had captured a bit of daylight. It hurt, and it made me weak. The light only lasted a few seconds, but it was long enough for the slayer to grab me and shove lavender in my mouth."

"Lavender?" I interrupted.

"It weakens vampires," Mori explained. "It's not as strong as sunlight, or as painful, but a little bit will reduce our strength to that of a human."

"I couldn't put up much of a fight, and the slayer bound my hands. I thought he was going to make me a prisoner, but instead, he"—Theo shut his eyes and laid one hand against his jaw—"filed my fangs down so I couldn't bite humans anymore. He said he was taming me. Then, he untied me and told me to warn any other vampires in the area they would be hunted down and killed, just like my five shipmates."

Even Damien looked unsettled by Theo's story. I wanted to wrap my arms around Theo in a great big hug, but before I could make a move, he suddenly smiled. "That's how I wound up here. I tried to continue on as a pirate, but I was so paranoid I never even left the ship to go ashore. Every night, as dawn approached, I worried our ship would be boarded by the hunter. I started hearing rumors there were safe havens for vampires in Virginia, so I went there. I traveled from one enclave to another, but I never found one that really felt like home, and eventually, I heard there was a place out West where all manner of supernatural creatures were welcome. It was a long and scary journey by train, but I made it. Baxter was sympathetic to my situation, and he told me I could join the Sanctuary family as long as I adhered to the rules."

"There are rules?" I asked. I was directing my question to Damien, who nodded emphatically.

"Like no killing humans," Mori supplied.

"Being here made me a better person. Er, vampire," Theo said. "I mesmerize tourists, like Mori does, so I can drink a bit of their blood, then send them off without a single memory of the event. Unlike Mori, though, I can't bite them." Theo pulled out a small pocketknife. "But this works."

"The vampire slayer used you to send a message," I said thoughtfully. "That means it's possible the girl who was killed at the saloon was meant to send a message, too, but would a slayer kill an innocent person?"

Three sets of shoulders shrugged. None of us knew enough to speculate.

"Theo, I'm sorry Justine and I brought Allie and Jon here," I said. "We didn't know you had been through something so awful. No wonder the idea of a vampire slayer is terrifying for you. I'm sure we can find somewhere else for them to stay, somewhere safe."

Theo gave me a small smile. "No. The Sanctuary is the safest place in Nightmare for a vampire or any other supernatural creature. If Allie really is a target, then she needs to be here. I'll find somewhere else to lay low. I'm actually thinking of asking if there's room for me to crash at Under the Undertaker's. The bar isn't open during the day, when I'm asleep, so I shouldn't be in the way."

"I'll drive you," Damien said. "You, too, Olivia. I'm not letting either one of you walk around at night when there's a killer—maybe even a vampire slayer—on the loose."

I was usually up for an argument with Damien, but in this case, I one hundred percent agreed with him. Mori wished us good luck and a good night, I patted Felipe on the head, and soon, I was crammed into the back seat of Damien's silver Corvette.

We drove to Under the Undertaker's first. The entrance to the basement-level bar was in an alley behind High Noon Boulevard, and Damien eased his car slowly between the buildings and the row of trash bins opposite them. While Theo got out and walked to the door of the bar for supernaturals, I un-pretzeled myself from the back seat and climbed into the passenger seat.

A moment later, Theo turned around and walked back to the car. "No answer," he said, frowning. "They're always open at night."

"They're probably as scared as everyone else," I speculated. "Plus, if every supernatural creature in Nightmare is staying in tonight because of this murder, they wouldn't get any business, anyway. There's no point for them to be open." I sighed as I got out of the car and returned to the back seat, my knees up under my chin.

"Do we have a Plan B?" Damien asked.

"Theo, you can stay at my apartment," I suggested. "I have windows, but I can cover them up with something."

"No. Absolutely not," Damien said resolutely.

"Why not?" I asked.

Damien's fingers curled tightly around the steering wheel. "It's not a good idea. It's dangerous, for you and for Theo."

Apparently, that was all I was going to get out of Damien for an explanation. I thought it seemed like a silly excuse, because it would be dangerous for Theo anywhere, and I would be awake during the day to keep an eye out. I considered saying as much to Damien, but instead, I got an even better idea. "Sonny's Folly!"

"What?" Theo asked. He twisted around to peer at me from the front seat.

"Damien, what if Theo hides in the mine your father owns? You can break the lock on the door." As a matter of fact, I had been telling Damien since I found out Baxter owned Sonny's Folly Mine that he should break the rusted old padlock and go inside. After all, I had heard what was, apparently, Baxter's voice coming from the mine. Damien, however, was convinced his missing father wasn't inside, and that what I had heard had been tied to my so-called conjuring skills.

Remember what I said about usually being up for an argument with Damien? We had been fighting about it for weeks now.

"Baxter owns a mine?" Theo asked, glancing from me to Damien.

Damien sighed deeply. Whether he was doing it to keep himself from getting angry or to still his mind while he debated the idea, I didn't know. Eventually, though, the car began moving forward slowly. "We'll organize some of our people who can handle daylight to watch over you while you sleep. It won't be comfortable. It's a mine, so you'll be sleeping on a hard rock floor, though we can bring a mattress over for you."

Theo waved a hand. "I'm not picky. When the sun rises, I'm basically dead to the world. I've slept on bare rock before, and it's no problem."

None of us spoke on the drive to the edge of Nightmare, where there was a low hill with an iron door leading into Sonny's Folly Mine. Damien seemed to grow more tense as we drove, but I didn't realize I was, too, until Theo slid a hand back and touched my leg. "Olivia, calm down." I had been bouncing my leg nervously, smacking the back of Theo's seat.

There were no streetlights on the narrow, little-used road that led past the mine, so when we pulled up and climbed out of the car, it took a moment for my eyes to adjust to the surroundings. At first, the only way I could tell where the hill ended and the sky began was the fact there were stars twinkling in the sky.

Damien produced his cell phone and used the flashlight function to shine a beam of light at the padlock on the door to the mine. Theo had lost his fangs, but he still had the super strength that came with being a vampire. He curled his fingers around the lock, yanked hard, and it snapped open. The metal creaked as he worked the lock off the door and pushed down on the handle.

The door opened inward, the hinges squealing and grating after decades of disuse. The three of us huddled in the doorway, facing the utterly black space beyond.

"Well," Theo said with forced levity, "at least I don't have to worry about daylight getting in."

Damien raised his cell phone, but the flashlight was nearly useless in the dark. Until, at least, he turned his phone to the side, illuminating a light switch next to the door. Even while telling myself there was no way the mine had power, I reached out and flicked the dusty switch.

I heard the low hum of sodium lights, then, one by one, lights blinked on overhead.

We were standing in a living room.

CHAPTER FIVE

The couch, chairs, and coffee table we were staring at were covered with white dust cloths, making them look like a sort of ghostly furniture arrangement. The cloths were coated in a layer of dust, dirt, and pebbles shaken loose from the ceiling of the mine over the years. The woven rug under the coffee table had probably been bright and pretty once, and maybe it would be again after a thorough cleaning.

Framed black-and-white photos hung on the walls, if you could call them walls. Their dull, mottled red surface was rough and angular, showing the hews of cutting tools once used to bore tunnels and extract copper from the mine.

My mouth was hanging open in utter shock. I was sure Damien had a similar expression, but I couldn't tear my eyes away from the scene in front of me to look at him. The three of us stood there in silence until Theo said happily, "Wow! This is great! Who knew this mine was a house?"

Damien was standing close to me, and I felt the way he shook himself. "Who knew?" he repeated.

Theo was already moving forward, and he slowly pulled the dust cover off the couch, being careful to roll it into itself so the mess on top was contained. The couch underneath was upholstered in a floral-patterned material. The brown and orange tones looked like they came from the same era as the orange shag rug in my apartment.

Theo uncovered the two chairs next. They were well worn, but the pale brown leather still had a faint gleam. Theo sank down into one of the chairs and sighed happily. "I can't wait to see what else is in this mine! There might be an actual bed I can sleep in!"

"You said you didn't know your father owned a mine until I told you," I said to Damien. "You didn't live here as a kid?"

"I grew up at the Sanctuary. I have no idea why my father owns something like this."

"Want to help Theo look for a bedroom?" I asked. I was resisting the urge to run headlong down the tunnel to explore every nook and cranny. It was dark beyond the makeshift living room, but I assumed we would find more light switches.

Damien, though, shook his head and took a step back. "No. Let's do it later."

"But," I began, then stopped. Damien had a look on his face that I could only describe as dread. I wasn't sure why, but it seemed that while I was eager to learn Baxter's secrets, he preferred to stay in the dark about them. "Okay," I said gently. "It's late, and we've all had a very long night. We'll leave Theo to get settled in."

Theo seemed oblivious to Damien's distress as he tossed his duffel bag onto the couch. "This is great! I'm going to unpack my stuff and look around a bit."

I wished Theo a good night after we checked to make sure the door could be locked from the inside. Once Damien and I were in his car, I had to press my lips together to keep from asking the many questions running through my mind. Damien, I suspected, wanted silence.

When Damien dropped me off at the foot of the stairs

leading up to my apartment, he didn't say a word. He did, however, wait until I had shut the door before pulling away.

So much had happened during the evening that I was surprised to look at the clock on my nightstand and see it wasn't even midnight yet. Since I normally worked until that hour, it wasn't even my bedtime. Still, after I had snacked on some leftovers and washed my face, I was ready to fall into bed.

On Tuesday morning, I got up feeling refreshed. It was a new day, and, if I were lucky, this one wouldn't have any murders in it. Plus, while the Sanctuary was closed on Mondays, each of us got a second night off, too. I was free on Tuesdays, and I liked having the back-to-back nights off, since it made Monday and Tuesday like my weekend.

After my second cup of coffee, I decided to head up to the front office. Gossip about the murder would have reached Mama already, and I expected she would be eager to hear a firsthand account. Since she was one of the "normal" people of Nightmare who didn't know about the supernatural community, I couldn't share the fears that the killer was a vampire slayer, but I could give her the rest of the details, at least.

But when I walked through the glass front door of the office, I didn't see Mama's puff of wavy gray hair sticking up above the Formica countertop. Instead, I saw the top of a man's head. His hair was gray, too, but it was combed flat against his head to help hide a bald spot right on top.

The man stood up from the chair behind the counter and smiled at me, his gray eyes twinkling. I immediately knew this had to be Mama's husband, because he looked so much like their son, Nick.

I grinned back at the man. I couldn't help it. Like his wife and his son, he exuded a feeling of warmth and friendliness. "Benny Dalton?" I said.

"In the flesh! I'm finally back from Phoenix. And you're Olivia. Mama told me to keep an eye out for a pretty woman with auburn hair and a smile that could light up a room."

I felt my cheeks flush at the unexpected compliment. I couldn't remember the last time someone had called me pretty. Probably my ex-husband, and probably back in my early thirties. "How's your uncle over in Phoenix? He must be doing better since you're finally back."

Benny pointed upward. "He's upstairs now."

"Oh, did he come back with you?" I asked. The white cinderblock office building had a second story, which housed an efficiency apartment, similar to mine.

"No, I mean he's in Heaven. He died."

My cheeks flushed again. "I am so, so sorry. My condolences."

Benny waved a hand toward me. "Thank you, but don't be embarrassed. Uncle Phil was old. He had a good, long life, and he had an easy transition."

"We should all hope for the same," I said sincerely.

"Indeed. But neither you nor I are on our deathbeds just yet, which means you'll probably be able to have lunch with my Susie. If you're up for it, she'd like to meet you at The Lusty Lunch Counter at noon."

I smiled. "Sure. I'll call her and tell her I'll be there." After a few more minutes of pleasant conversation with Benny, I walked back to my apartment. Even as I pulled out my cell phone—well, it was really Baxter's, but Damien had loaned it to me until his dad turned up—to call Mama, I wondered why she hadn't simply invited me to lunch herself rather than relying on Benny to pass along the message.

Because she knew you'd walk up to the front office this morning.

I knew I was right, but that left the question of whether Mama just knew my habits that well already, or if she was somehow psychic. I already knew she tended to get impressions from people—vibes, as I thought of them—that were eerily accurate. Maybe she could see the future, too.

My deal with Mama was that I got to stay in the apartment for free in exchange for doing marketing work for Cowboy's Corral Motor Lodge. After I called her to confirm our lunch plans, I spent the remainder of the morning sitting at my kitchen table, hunched over the bulky old laptop Mama had loaned me for the job.

Occasionally, I resented the fact so much of what I had was secondhand or only on loan. I had bought the cheapest used car I could find, my cell phone and laptop were loaners, and my apartment hadn't been stylish since the nineteen sixties, at least.

Then again, I reminded myself, I had new friends who made me feel accepted and cared for, no matter how broke I was or what circumstances had landed me in Nightmare. I'd put up with all the secondhand technology in the world for that sense of belonging.

When I walked to The Lusty Lunch Counter, I took side streets so I could avoid High Noon Boulevard. For one thing, I didn't feel like elbowing my way past tourists. Mostly, though, it was because I didn't want to get so much as a peek at the saloon. Even though I would be comfortable sharing the news with Mama, I didn't need the visual reminder of everything that had happened the night before.

Mama was already seated at a booth when I walked inside The Lusty. On the outside, the place was a dilapidated clapboard building that looked like it belonged in a Wild West ghost town, complete with a high front facade and a lopsided front balcony. Inside the former brothel, though, The Lusty looked like a classic diner, with rows of booths and a long stainless steel counter lined with stools.

I settled onto the red cushioned bench seat across from

Mama. My friend Ella bustled over with a diet soda and put it in front of me. She usually served customers seated at the counter, and when I pointed that out to her, she said cheerfully, "It just doesn't feel right if I'm not the one to hand you a soda."

"Thanks, Ella." Once she headed back to the serving area behind the counter, I turned my attention to Mama. "I finally got to meet your husband!"

Mama grinned. "I thought about telling you he was back in town, but I didn't want to ruin the surprise." She leaned forward over the table and dropped her voice. "You were planning to go to the saloon last night. Did you see anything?"

"I sure did." Unlike Mama, I didn't bother to lower my voice. I was sure all of Nightmare already knew the details, so there was no point being discreet. I filled Mama in on the curtain rising to reveal a dead saloon girl, and the wooden stake that had practically seemed to gleam under the glare of the spotlight.

Mama shook her head when I was finished. "I didn't know Kelly Lowry, but I can't imagine why anyone would murder her right in the middle of the stage like that."

"I didn't even know her name, and I was there. You definitely got the detailed gossip."

"Her name is larger than life on the front page of this morning's newspaper."

We chatted about the murder for a few more minutes, before Mama turned the subject to Damien. "I saw his car at the motel yesterday. Again."

I would never understand why Mama liked the idea of me spending time with Damien. She knew he could be the world's biggest jerk, but she seemed to think there was a heart of gold under the rude exterior.

The muscular, tanned, rude exterior.

By the time we finished eating and paid, we had—

thankfully—moved on to subjects like the beginning of the school year and when it would start feeling like fall. In my limited experience, Arizona didn't seem to have any season other than *Hot and Miserable*.

Mama was heading to the grocery store, and after she left, I made a beeline for the door to the kitchen. I had to walk behind the counter, but Ella waved me through. The owner of The Lusty, Jeff Crosley, had a small office in one corner of the kitchen. His door was open, and I could see him working at the desk he had crammed into the tiny space.

"Hi, Jeff," I said, poking my head into the office.

"Olivia, hey." Jeff smiled up at me.

I decided to get right to business. "I'm sure you've heard about the murder at the saloon. Do you know if there's a vampire slayer in town?"

Jeff stood abruptly and leaned past me so he could look around the kitchen. "Don't say that so loud," he hissed. Jeff was a retired monster hunter. There had been a time in his life when he had gone after supernatural creatures like my friends, but I was working hard not to hold that against him. He had, after all, helped solve a murder Ella had been framed for.

"Sorry," I whispered.

No one was in earshot, anyway, and Jeff relaxed. "Slayers are extremely rare." I nodded. Mori had said the same thing. "And remember, hunters hide their work. They wouldn't kill in front of an audience."

"True," I agreed, "but we need to consider every option."

"This wasn't the work of a slayer," Jeff said, shaking his head. "It wasn't even a proper stake. The murder weapon was just a broken pool cue."

CHAPTER SIX

I frowned. "A pool cue?" The murder suddenly sounded like a bar fight gone wrong rather than any kind of planned attack. "How do you know?"

Jeff threw back his balding head and laughed. "Olivia, I own the only diner in Nightmare. Every single piece of worthy gossip comes through my front door."

"Between your diner being the top gathering place in Nightmare and your, shall we say, prior career experience, you're definitely at the top of my list of people to speak to whenever anything odd happens." I gave Jeff a lopsided smile.

"As long as Baxter's collection of creatures behave, then I'm happy to help." Jeff said it affably enough, but I could sense the veiled threat.

I thanked Jeff and turned to go, but I stopped and said, "Wait a minute. There aren't any pool tables at the saloon. I was thinking this might have been a spur-of-the-moment killing, maybe even an accident, but someone had to bring that pool cue into the saloon with them."

"That's right, though I still say a vampire slayer would have used a real stake rather than a pool cue."

"Whether it was a slayer behind this or not, someone showed up at the saloon with the murder weapon. I'd like to find out where they got it from, because it might help us track down some answers."

Jeff looked down at his desk. "Let me think," he said slowly. "The Neon Coyote has pool tables. Where else? Oh, yeah, I think they also have them at Bank Notes."

At my look of utter confusion, Jeff clarified, "It's a blues bar in an old bank, way down on the south end of town. Back when the mine was still giving copper and this place was a true Wild West town, the bank on High Noon Boulevard got robbed. After that, Nightmare's mayor decided they should have two banks positioned as far away from each other as possible. That way, if one of them got robbed, there would still be something left at the other bank."

"Did some enterprising outlaw ever try to rob both?" I asked.

"Legend says that none other than Butch Tanner was going to attempt it, but his plans were discovered before he could pull it off."

I smiled. Butch Tanner was Nightmare's most famous outlaw. He and Nightmare's sheriff, Connor McCrory, had killed each other in a shootout right in the middle of High Noon Boulevard. Every day, costumed actors recreated it for eager tourists. Even though the shootout had happened in the late eighteen hundreds, I made a mental note to ask Tanner if the legend about the banks was true. He and McCrory were both residents at the Sanctuary, albeit as ghosts.

"Thanks for the info, Jeff," I said. "I'm going to pass along the news that we're probably looking at an old-fashioned, not-supernatural murder."

"I'll let you know if any significant rumors reach my ears."

I walked home, only to get inside my front door and realize I was awfully sweaty. *So much for fall weather,* I thought as I stripped off my T-shirt. I needed another shower, and it was only two o'clock in the afternoon.

Once I was showered and dressed in a burgundy sundress, I drove to the Sanctuary while mentally thanking Nick Dalton for having not only fixed my car when I broke down outside of Nightmare, but for making the air-conditioner work exceptionally well.

Zach was standing outside the front double doors of the Sanctuary. The doors were recessed in the building's facade, so at least Zach was in the shade. Despite the heat, he was dressed in his usual tight blue jeans and a threadbare T-shirt. His thick, rust-red hair had been pulled back into what I think was supposed to be a bun. To me, it looked more like a rat's nest, but I wasn't about to tell him that.

"Hey, Zach," I called as I walked up to him. "It looks like we might not be dealing with a vampire slayer, after all."

"'Might not' means it still might be," Zach said grumpily. "We're not calling off the extra security detail until we know for sure, so I can kiss sleep goodbye for the foreseeable future."

I flashed a big smile at Zach. "It's nice to see you, too," I said cheerily. Zach was rarely in a good mood, partly because he only got to enjoy his supernatural side during the three days a month the moon was full. On every other day, he was the Sanctuary's accountant, ticket seller, and—since Baxter's disappearance—security guard. He didn't seem to like any of those jobs very much, though I could see how they might seem boring in comparison to being a werewolf.

One of the front doors opened and Gunnar's massive form appeared. He ducked so his head wouldn't hit the doorframe, and he had to turn slightly sideways so his wings would fit through. Once he was outside, he rolled his shoulders back, and his sinewy, batlike wings flexed, unfurling about halfway. Gunnar's gray skin had a greenish tone to it, like moss growing on stone. He gave me a sharp-toothed smile, then said to Zach, "Your watch is done. Go get some rest."

Zach turned and disappeared through the door, grumbling something about balancing an account as he went.

"You know," Gunnar said conversationally to me, "some legends say gargoyles turn to stone in the daylight, and we only come to life at sunset."

"Would you rather be stone right now, or doing security duty?"

"My kind were made for keeping guard. Why do you think there are so many statues of us on old European churches? We keep the bad things at bay."

"I do feel safe whenever I'm with you," I said honestly. "I came here to share news about the murder. I told Zach already, but he's being antisocial and may not spread the word." I filled Gunnar in on the murder weapon and the unlikeliness of a slayer being in Nightmare, and he promised he would pass it along. Inside, I knew most of those who lived at the Sanctuary were asleep, so he would wait until they woke up that night to fill everyone in.

Since my visit to the Sanctuary had been so brief, I figured I should stop by the mine, as well, to see how Theo was doing. He, too, would be asleep, but I could at least have a chat with whomever was standing guard there.

I was surprised when I pulled over to the side of the road right in front of the mine and didn't see anyone at the door. I was instantly worried, and I turned off my car and climbed out as quickly as I could. When I reached the door, I pressed my ear against it. The last time I had done that, I had heard a man's voice on the other side, uttering a phrase Damien told me his father used to say when he felt like his authority was being threatened.

This time, I didn't hear anything, so I cautiously grabbed the door handle and pulled. The lights were on in the living room, but I didn't see any sign of Theo. Instead, I saw Damien sitting on the couch, a laptop on the coffee table in front of him. He was leaning forward with his hands braced on the cushions, looking in my direction.

"It's just me," I said, walking inside. I instinctively raised my hands in surrender. Damien had an intensity to his gaze, even when his eyes *weren't* glowing.

Damien didn't relax. "What are you doing here?" he asked warily.

I closed and bolted the door behind me. "Why was the door unlocked?" I countered.

"I guess I forgot to do it earlier."

"Then it's a good thing I'm not a vampire slayer."

Damien shut his eyes and pinched the bridge of his nose with two fingers. "So you came here to tell me I'm doing this bodyguard thing all wrong."

There was something off about Damien. I couldn't put my finger on what, but clearly, something was bothering him. Well, something other than me. That was a given. I looked at him closely. He looked tense, and his hair was disheveled. It looked like he had been running his fingers through it.

Is he nervous? I wondered. *Afraid? No, if he was afraid, he would have double-checked the bolt on the door.* When Mama had made Damien watch over me one night, he had been incredibly vigilant. He had stayed awake all night, posted right in front of my door to make sure no one could get in.

"Damien," I said. When he looked up at me, I opened my mouth, but nothing came out. I wasn't even sure what I had planned to say. I swallowed hard as Damien gazed at me expectantly, and I thought back to the look I had seen on his face when we had come inside the mine the night before. Dread.

I walked slowly to the couch and sank down next to him. "It's this place, isn't it?" I asked. "It's upsetting you."

Damien stared at me, expressionless, but his mouth tightened, ever so slightly.

"It's okay," I said hastily, waving my hands. "Never mind. I'm not going to pry. I just came to check on things here, and obviously, you and Theo are safe, so I'll be on my way."

I stood, not even looking at Damien, but I had only taken one step when his hand grabbed mine, and I turned to him in surprise. Damien took a deep breath, then said, "It's not just this place, but something in it." He dropped my hand and stood, turning toward the tunnel that led deeper into the mine.

Either Damien or Theo had found the switch for the lights that marched down the length of the main tunnel, which branched into two smaller tunnels about a hundred feet ahead of us. I followed Damien down the tunnel, and I saw there were doors along it. The red paint on them was peeling, and some of the wood was gouged. Damien stopped about halfway down the main tunnel, in front of a door that sagged on its hinges. He had to push the door with his shoulder to get it open, and it grated loudly against the rock floor.

"The light in here isn't working," Damien explained as he pulled out his cell phone and used the flashlight function on it again.

We were clearly in a bedroom, because there was an iron bed frame with a thin mattress covered by a white sheet. A small dresser stood against the far wall. As Damien's light swept across it, I could see there were a few items on top of it, including what looked like a jewelry box and a cut-crystal bowl with an elegant lid.

Damien reached forward and grasped a photo frame that was propped on the dresser. He shined his light onto a photo of a woman wearing a sleeveless plaid dress. Even though the colors had faded with time, I could see she had gorgeous green eyes. Her dark hair was feathered. The photo had to be from the nineteen seventies, I figured.

"Look at her necklace," Damien said, his voice barely above a whisper.

I gasped, my fingers instinctively reaching up to touch my own necklace, a silver chain with two small charms: a cross and a pentagram.

Not my necklace, I thought. *Hers.*

"Oh, Damien," I said breathlessly. "This is your mother."

CHAPTER SEVEN

Damien slowly put the framed photo back in its place on the dresser. He kept his eyes fixed on it as he said, "I know. I've never seen a photo of her before, but this must be my mother. That's her necklace."

"And your eyes," I said. "You got your green eyes from her."

"I wonder..." Damien reached a finger toward the dusty glass covering the photo.

He didn't finish his sentence, but I knew there were a lot of things he must be wondering about. Did her eyes glow when she was angry or upset, too? Had she been supernatural, and if so, in what way?

There was another question that seemed even more important than those, so I said, "What happened to her? You said you never knew her, and that your dad always refused to talk about her."

"I assume she died, but I don't know how or when." Damien turned to me, the look of dread finally gone from his face. Instead, he looked resigned, almost sad. "Just another mystery about my father."

"Maybe they lived here before you were born," I suggested. "You said you grew up at the Sanctuary, but Baxter bought this mine before you were born. Perhaps he bought it with the intention of living in it."

"Maybe. If that's true, then it raises even more questions. Tanner and McCrory couldn't get in here because this mine is lined on every side with iron. We had speculated iron panels were installed to secure the mine from robbers, long before my father bought it, but it's just paint. As far as I can figure, every surface of this mine was coated with an iron-rich paint of some kind. It's why the walls are red. The iron filings in the paint have rusted. If my father did it, then why? Why would he want to keep ghosts out?"

I turned and looked around the room, but in the dim light from Damien's cell phone flashlight, I couldn't make out a lot of details. "Tanner and McCrory are good guys. Well, one was an outlaw during his lifetime, but they're harmless as ghosts. Baxter might have built this to ward off an unwanted ghost. A violent one, perhaps."

"Come on," Damien said, heading for the door. "I know you're dying to see the rest of this place, so let's go."

It didn't take long for Damien to give me a tour of the rest of the mine. At the fork, we turned right, but that stretch of tunnel was only about fifty feet long. It ended in a plaster wall with a door in it. "The end of the tunnel was enclosed to create another bedroom," Damien explained. "Theo's sleeping in there. There's no way daylight can get in, and the bed has the best mattress."

We retraced our steps and took the left-hand tunnel. It was slightly longer, but there were no doors leading off it, and the string of overhead lights ended about halfway down. "I guess Baxter never got around to renovating this part," I mused. "Of course, he wouldn't have needed even more bedrooms unless he and your mother were planning to have a lot of kids."

As I spoke, I continued walking toward the dark end of the tunnel. When I reached it, I put out a hand to touch the cold rock. Something sharp pricked the tip of my index finger, and I yanked my hand back. "Ow!" I instinctively stuck my finger into my mouth, and I could taste blood.

Damien shined his flashlight against the wall, and he leaned so far forward the tip of his nose nearly touched the rock. "It's a spike. A silver spike, needle thin." He moved the flashlight across the face of the wall. "There are more. Someone put silver spikes into the walls of the mine."

I took my finger out of my mouth. It still stung, but it wasn't bleeding anymore. "If the iron was used to ward off ghosts and fairies," I said, "then the silver might be werewolf repellent. Again, though, why?"

Damien shook his head. "Dad took care of supernatural creatures. Why would he feel the need to protect his home from them?"

I had noticed Damien switched from saying "my father" to "dad" on the rare occasions he dropped his resentment toward Baxter. I was sure he was thinking the same thing I was as I said, "What kind of trouble was your dad in back then?"

"Add it to the list of questions," Damien said.

We returned to the living room, but instead of sitting down on the couch again, Damien walked to the door and opened it. Clearly, he was ready for me to leave. I wanted to say something comforting, but I couldn't find the right words. Instead, I told Damien to call me if he needed anything, and I left.

My plan was to spend the afternoon working on a new brochure for the motel. The current one had been made fifteen years before, and it was looking woefully out of date. It was fine for the motel itself to revel in its retro kitsch, but not the marketing materials that went with it. I sat down at my dining room table with the laptop and a big glass of diet soda, planning to knock out the brochure in just a couple of hours.

I had been working on the same sentence for thirty

minutes when I realized I wasn't getting anywhere. My mind was too busy thinking about the murder at the saloon and the strange discoveries at the mine. With a huff, I slammed the laptop lid shut and stood. I put on my shoes and took the laptop up to the front office, figuring that if I was working in a room with someone else, then maybe I would be more productive. After all, I didn't want Mama to catch me staring off into space when I was supposed to be earning my keep. I settled into one of the sagging faux-leather chairs in the lobby, right next to the pot of weak, slightly burnt coffee Mama kept going all day for guests.

I had finally gotten past the first sentence of the brochure—in fact, I had written an entire paragraph—when the bell on the front door of the office tinkled wildly. I looked up to see Mama's granddaughter, Lucy, bursting through the door. That kid was always full of energy, and I was a bit envious. It had been a couple of decades since I had been that bubbly and bouncy.

Lucy shouted a hello to Mama, then turned and saw me. She ran over, her pink light-up sneakers flashing with each step and her thick, dark curls bouncing. "Miss Olivia! Hey!" Lucy shouted, throwing her arms around me so violently that the laptop was in danger of falling to the floor. I hugged her back with one arm while grabbing the laptop with the other.

"I started school yesterday," Lucy said proudly as she let go of me and stepped back. She straightened her pink T-shirt, which had an image of a cartoon unicorn on it, and puffed out her chest proudly. "I'm in the fourth grade now, which means next year will be my last year at Nightmare Elementary. Then I'll be in middle school."

"I'm guessing your dad isn't as excited about you growing up so fast," I said, even as I saw Nick walk through the door. He moved at a much slower pace than his daughter. For once, Nick wasn't in the usual oil-stained white overalls he wore when working at his shop, Done Right Auto Repair. Instead, he was wearing khaki pants and a white short-sleeved Oxford shirt. I peered at him closely, and I couldn't spot a single oil stain on him.

"Hi, Nick," I called. Nick returned the greeting as he walked behind the counter to give his mother a peck on the cheek. I turned my attention back to Lucy, who was moving her feet in a little dance. "Did you learn that at school?" I asked her.

"Yeah. All the girls in my grade are doing it. Hey, I saw that one girl again. The bad one."

I fought to keep the smile on my face. "You mean the girl on the playground?" I asked as casually as I could.

"Uh-huh. She was standing over by the swings, staring at me. I wanted to ask her what her problem was, so I told my friend Katelyn to come with me. But when I looked again, she was gone. I guess she saw the look on my face and knew I meant business. No one messes with Lucy Dalton!"

I laughed at Lucy's self-confidence, but at the same time, I suppressed a shudder. Lucy had mentioned the "bad-feeling girl" before. Just like the last time, Lucy had spotted the girl on the playground, staring. And, again, Lucy had looked away, during which time the girl mysteriously disappeared.

I knew it was a ghost Lucy had seen, but I wasn't about to break that news to her. I wondered if the other kids on the playground had seen the ghost, too, or if it was only Lucy who had that gift.

Damien would call it a curse, I thought.

I glanced toward Mama and Nick, but the two of them were talking to each other, oblivious to what Lucy had just told me. That was a relief, since Mama had seemed unhappy with Lucy's first report of seeing the ghost girl, and I quickly changed the subject with Lucy, asking her about her favorite subjects in school.

After a few minutes of chatting, Mama called my name, and I looked up. "We're going to an early dinner," she said. "Benny is going to mind things here until the office closes for the night. Would you like to join us?"

"Of course!" I said immediately. "How early are we talking?" The sun hadn't even set yet.

"In an hour. Nick and Lucy are going to run a few quick errands for me. We'll head out around five."

I agreed, and after Nick and Lucy had left with a shopping list from Mama, I managed to finish up the motel brochure in only thirty minutes. Thinking about dinner and good company had finally pushed murder and the mine out of my head, and I could concentrate.

By the time five o'clock rolled around, the day was feeling less hot. When we met up for dinner, Nick squinted his faded blue eyes and said knowingly, "Fall is nearly here. Nights are going to start getting a lot cooler."

I hoped he was right. I had sweated more in the past month than I had in all my years in Nashville. Hot and humid I was used to. Hot and dry? Not so much.

Since it was shaping up to be a pleasant evening, we walked to dinner. The entrance to the restaurant was off a short alley at the far end of High Noon Boulevard, between the Nightmare History Museum and dilapidated horse stables that had been turned into a gardening store. The Red Stagecoach was so tucked away I hadn't even known it existed, but everyone else sure knew it was there. By the time we finished our dinner, the restaurant was packed.

We left the restaurant with full bellies, and Mama suggested we stroll down High Noon Boulevard rather than hightailing it back to the motel. We had made it about halfway down the street when I spotted a small crowd of people on the boardwalk to our right. As we got closer, I realized they were standing in front of the saloon.

My heart beat wildly as I worried there had been another murder. As we got closer, I could see that wasn't true. I spotted several photos of a blonde woman in her twenties, bouquets of flowers, and lit seven-day candles arranged next to the saloon entrance. It was a small memorial to the woman who had been staked. A man stood to one side of it, addressing the crowd at what was obviously a vigil.

"Thank you for coming," the man said, his voice cracking. "Kelly would have been so happy to see how many people loved her. Your outpouring of support has meant so much. She was the best girlfriend a guy could ask for." The man fell silent, bit his lip, and bowed his head.

When he turned toward the memorial, I could see the back of his black leather jacket. A patch covered the back, featuring a cartoonish yellow coyote surrounded by the words *Neon Coyote Motorcycle Club*.

CHAPTER EIGHT

I immediately thought of my conversation with Jeff at The Lusty, when he had said there were only two places in Nightmare that had pool tables. One of them was The Neon Coyote, the biker bar that was on the main road through Nightmare, just a few blocks down from Cowboy's Corral. I had passed the neon-yellow coyote statue in front of the bar dozens of times on my treks to and from The Lusty Lunch Counter.

Mama elbowed me lightly. "You okay?"

I finally stopped staring at the jacket and its wearer so I could give Mama a quizzical look. "How did you know?"

"You stopped right in the middle of the boardwalk, and I had to take evasive action to avoid plowing into you," Mama said with a chuckle. "It doesn't take a psychic to figure out you're mulling over something important."

I lowered my voice so Lucy wouldn't overhear. "The woman at the saloon—Kelly, right?—was killed with a broken pool cue. Only two places in town have pool tables, and her boyfriend is wearing a jacket for one of them."

"Oh, you think the boyfriend killed her?" Mama didn't bother to lower her voice, and a man at the edge of the assembled group of mourners spun around to stare at us with a horrified expression. I quickly averted my eyes, but

Mama waved at the man. "Hey, Orin, good to see you! A shame about this murder, isn't it?"

Mama walked toward the man and was soon chatting easily with him, so I let my attention return to the boyfriend. He was moving slowly in our direction, hugging or shaking hands with people. When he got closer to me, he hesitated, then closed the distance between us and stuck out a hand. "Hi, I don't think we've met. Miguel Fernandez."

I shook Miguel's hand, taking in his unshaven face and disheveled dark hair. I could tell he was handsome under ordinary circumstances. Even the jagged scar across his chin, just peeking out from under his stubble, added to his good looks. It made him look slightly mysterious. Suddenly aware that I was staring, I dropped my hand and introduced myself. "I'm sorry for your loss," I added, even while wondering if I was talking to the person who had killed Kelly.

And, I suddenly realized, if he had killed Kelly, then did that mean Miguel was a vampire slayer? Maybe he had been trying to warn Allie. Instead of killing her outright, he had sent a message that she needed to leave Nightmare and never come back.

But, then, why would Miguel kill his own girlfriend? Had he never loved her to begin with? Maybe killing her had been part of his plot from the start, and he had planned this ever since Allie's last appearance in Nightmare.

Stop it, Liv. You're jumping to wild conclusions. I was also staring again. I cleared my throat self-consciously and asked, "How long were you and Kelly together?"

"Almost eight months."

Ah-ha! So he did start dating Kelly after Allie was last here!

"Have you always lived in Nightmare?" I asked.

Something like a smile appeared briefly on Miguel's face. "I'm third-generation Nightmare."

I needed to figure out a way to find out if Miguel was a slayer without asking him outright. Because, if he wasn't, it would sure seem like a bizarre question. I blurted, "A funny name, Nightmare. Does it mean there are monsters lurking in the dark around here?"

"It's called that because living here was such a nightmare in the early days. No air-conditioning, limited water, all supplies had to be brought in by wagons, that sort of thing. Life was hard for the miners."

"Oh. So it's not called Nightmare because there are vampires stalking the streets, then." I tried to sound as flippant as I could, and Miguel frowned as he shook his head.

"I mean, if you believe in those kinds of things," I continued. "Probably just creatures of legend, right? Do you believe in vampires?"

This time, Miguel took half a step back. "Of course not. If you'll excuse me, I need to say thank you to the others before they leave."

"Right. Sorry. Okay." I couldn't blame Miguel for turning on his heel and walking away in a hurry. I would have done the same thing if I had been in his shoes. I had gone and made the whole thing totally weird and awkward, when the poor guy was probably innocent and grieving.

Still, I told myself that even though Miguel claimed not to believe in vampires, that didn't take him off my suspect list. It would have been ridiculous if he had answered me with an affirmative. How would that conversation even have gone? "Yes, Olivia, I do believe in vampires. In fact, I slay them!"

I wasn't embarrassed by my questions. I just felt silly. I should have known better. If Kelly had been killed by a vampire slayer, I certainly wasn't going to find out by asking vague questions of the people in her circle.

Mama had wrapped up her conversation with the man she knew, so she and I both returned to Nick and Lucy, who were standing a short distance away. A woman had joined them. She looked to be about forty, making her just a bit younger than both Nick and me. And, judging by her thick, dark curls, she had to be Lucy's mom.

"Hi," I said hesitantly as I walked up.

The woman smiled at me. "You're Olivia, right? Lucy has been going on and on about you. I'm Mia."

"You're," I said, looking from Mia to Nick, "Lucy's mom, right?"

Nick laughed. "Half the people in this town think my name is 'Mia's husband,' so I'm happy to know she's just 'Lucy's mom.'"

"You're married?" I said it before I could stop myself. *Well, here comes my second awkward conversation of the evening.*

Mia glared at Nick, but I could also see the way one corner of her mouth turned up. "You never mentioned me?" she scolded him teasingly.

"He's mentioned you," I clarified. "I just didn't realize you two were married." How could I have known, though? I had only ever seen Nick by himself or with Lucy. I had assumed Nick was divorced.

Nick laughed. "I'm so used to everyone knowing that I guess I forgot to say anything. Mia works at a hair salon on the east side of town, and she's often there late for clients who can't come in until they get off work. So, in the evenings, it's usually just me and Lucy."

"As a matter of fact," Mia said, "Kelly was one of my clients. I came over for the vigil tonight to show my support."

That got my full attention. "What was she like?"

"You know how we all were in our early twenties. Big dreams, big drama."

"What kind of drama?" I asked. I wasn't sure if I was more surprised that Nick was married or that his wife was turning out to be an unexpected source of information in this murder.

"She kept talking about how she and Miguel were going to get married, and how they might just have to elope." Mia waved a hand airily, like she thought the whole thing was silly nonsense. "Kelly would tell me that, one day, I would wonder why she hadn't come in for a haircut in so long, and it would be because she had left town without telling anyone."

I could see why Mia had written it off as idle talk. It did, in fact, sound like the dreams of many small-town kids who wanted to get out and see a bit of the world. "Kelly's murder must be heartbreaking for Miguel if he was planning to spend the rest of his life with her."

"Just because she thought that was going to happen, doesn't mean he did, too," Mia noted. A thoughtful look came over her face, and she stared at a spot somewhere over my right shoulder. "Come to think of it…"

Even Mama and Nick leaned in eagerly. "What?" Mama prompted.

"Kelly was in for a trim just last week. She wasn't acting like her usual self. Gosh, I hadn't even thought about that until just now. I've been so focused on helping Lucy start off the school year that I forgot all about it. She seemed anxious, kind of jittery. She always talked a lot while she sat in my chair, but last week, it wasn't conversational. It was more like a constant babble."

"What kind of stuff was she babbling about?" I asked.

"She talked again about marrying Miguel, of course, and she complained how nosy everyone in this town is. The usual stuff. Kelly also mentioned wanting to take a road trip now that the weather was beginning to get cooler. None of it was anything shocking." Mia suddenly grinned at me. "Wait, are you trying to solve her murder? Nick mentioned it's a pastime of yours. Am I a witness in your investigation?"

I laughed self-consciously. "No. I mean, I'm as curious as everyone else to know who killed Kelly, and why, but I'm not a private investigator or anything."

Mia looked toward the memorial wistfully. "I wish I did have some useful information to share, but the stuff she was talking about last week was fairly routine for her."

Except, I thought, Mia had shared something incredibly useful. The fact Kelly had been acting nervous the week before meant she might have felt threatened at the time. And if that were the case, then neither Allie nor Jon were suspects since they hadn't arrived in Nightmare until Monday, the day of the show.

It also meant Allie was probably safe. The killer hadn't been a vampire slayer who accidentally staked the wrong person or was trying to send a message. Instead, it was just old-fashioned, small-town drama that culminated the night of Allie's show by pure coincidence. I remembered overhearing the bartender and the server the night of the murder, when the server had said Kelly had stolen from Frankie, the owner of the saloon. Perhaps that had led to Kelly's death.

I sighed, and I felt the tension drain out of my shoulders. Allie was safe. Theo and Mori were safe. And that meant this murder was none of my business. There was no need to keep prying into it.

Mia was parked one street over, and Lucy decided to go with her. We said good night, and I began walking with Mama and Nick in the direction of Cowboy's Corral. We had to pass the handful of people still milling about after the vigil, and I saw a heavyset woman with graying black hair fold Miguel into an embrace.

"My poor boy," she said. "It's been a long night. Let's get you home."

Miguel stepped back and wiped at his cheek. "Kelly said that singer was a vampire who would suck the life out of her, but I didn't think she was being literal."

CHAPTER NINE

It felt like my heart shot right up into my throat, but I forced my feet to keep going. We were past Miguel and his mother by then, and I didn't want to look back at them. It would be too obvious that I was eavesdropping. I had no way of knowing if Miguel was being literal, or if Kelly had somehow known Allie was a vampire. Maybe my conclusion that the murder didn't involve Allie or Jon had been wrong.

It was possible Kelly had been nervous during her haircut because she knew Allie's arrival in Nightmare was just days away, and she was terrified about having to be under the same roof with a vampire for a night.

My conversation with Miguel seemed even sillier in light of his comment to his mother. *Of course,* I chided myself. *Even if he wasn't a vampire slayer but simply someone who believed in vampires, he's not going to go around admitting that to people. It would seem absurd.*

I wasn't about to initiate another conversation with Miguel. At least, not anytime soon. Before talking to him again, I would have to come up with some kind of plan. I would need to know what I was going to say rather than winging it like I just had. Because that had absolutely not worked.

Instead, I promised myself I would talk to Frankie. I

could go to the saloon under the pretense of having a drink, then find a way to talk to him. If he seemed suspicious, then I could go back to the idea that Allie and Jon weren't involved in the murder in any way, either as targets or killers. As soon as I confirmed that, then I was done with this murder.

When we got back to the motel, Mama headed for her car—a red vintage Mustang that earned her a ton of cool points—and Nick climbed into his tow truck. I was halfway up the steps to my apartment when I realized someone was standing in front of my door. It was Mori, and Felipe was sitting at her feet.

"What's wrong?" I asked immediately. Mori had never been to my apartment before, and there was just something about her stance that told me something was going on.

"We'll talk inside," Mori said tightly.

I squeezed past her and Felipe, unlocked my door, and ushered them inside. It wasn't until I gestured for Mori to sit on the love seat that I realized she had a small suitcase in one hand. "Are you moving in?" I asked, surprised.

"For a while. If that's okay." Mori sank down onto the love seat, and Felipe hopped up onto her lap.

I slowly slid out of my shoes, suddenly feeling like an awful friend. "Justine and I should have never brought Allie back to the Sanctuary. First Theo refused to stay there with her, and now you."

"This isn't about Allie, or any danger she poses from an alleged vampire slayer." Mori shook her head. "It's her manager I'm not okay with."

I cocked my head in confusion. "Jon? He seems harmless."

"I don't like him. There's something off. He's so overly protective of her, following her around everywhere."

"To be fair, he's worried she might be a target."

Mori rolled her eyes. "She's at the Sanctuary. A slayer

isn't going to pop up in the middle of the dining room and stake her, especially when Zach has all of us taking turns doing security. That place is like a fort right now."

I sat down in one of the kitchen table chairs. "I'm sorry you don't feel safe in your own home, and I hate that it's because of me, in part. And yes, of course you can stay here."

"I don't blame you for all of this. You were just trying to help a vampire in need. I respect that. But I've stayed alive all these years because I listen to my intuition, and my intuition is telling me Jon is not someone to be around. Mind you, it might have nothing to do with that girl's murder."

"How is this going to work, then?" I asked, eager to change the subject to alleviate the guilt I was feeling. "It's nearly my bedtime, but your day is still young."

"Your bed is the safest spot for me to sleep during the day, since it's in an alcove with no windows. Maybe we can trade spots at daybreak?"

Ugh. That would require getting up way before I wanted to, but I didn't feel like I could say no, so I agreed.

"Also, do you have anything to cover the windows in here?" Mori continued. "Those curtains aren't thick enough for me to feel safe."

I thought for a moment. "I have a roll of aluminum foil. I could tape that over the windows."

"Perfect. And I have one more huge favor to ask." Mori looked sheepish. "Felipe will need to go out for a walk twice a day. He'll let you know when it's time. At the Sanctuary, he just uses the doggy door when I'm sleeping. Here, though, he'll need to be on his leash." Mori produced a purple dog leash from her suitcase.

I laughed. The chupacabra had a leash? I quickly sobered, though. "What am I supposed to tell anyone who stops and asks me what kind of dog he is?" I asked.

"Tell them he's a hairless greyhound."

"Come on, no one will believe that." *Especially,* I thought, *if Felipe starts walking on his hind legs.*

"You'd be surprised at what people will believe. To them, the idea of a hairless greyhound is a lot more logical than the idea a cryptid is trotting along the sidewalk on a leash."

"Do I have to feed him?" I felt grossed out at the thought.

"Don't worry. I'll handle that. He'll just want some water during the day."

That I could do. I got up and looked through the kitchen cupboards for a bowl that could double as a doggie dish. Or, in this case, a chupacabra dish. I pulled out a shallow pottery bowl with a gorgeous blue glaze that I had found at a yard sale. "How's this, Felipe?" I asked as I filled it with water at the kitchen sink.

Felipe slid off Mori's lap and came toward me with his tail wagging. I put the bowl on the floor, and before he bent down to drink, he looked up at me, his fangs bright against his leathery skin. It looked like he was smiling, which I always found simultaneously endearing and disturbing.

Something Mori had said suddenly clicked in my mind. "You don't seem to think Kelly's murder was the work of a vampire slayer."

"I'm more likely to get struck by lightning than to die at the hands of a slayer. I highly doubt there's one here in Nightmare."

"Jeff over at The Lusty shares your opinion. He says a slayer would have hidden their work, not done it right in the middle of a stage."

"He's right, but vampires also turn to dust when they're staked. A slayer wouldn't have expected there to be any evidence of their work, aside from a pile of dust. And this town has dust everywhere, so no one would have noticed."

That meant we couldn't completely rule out a slayer. I went to bed that night feeling out of sorts. Mori had settled onto the love seat with a book, and Felipe was happily dozing next to her. The lamp on the table next to Mori was on, but it wasn't the light that was bothering me. Instead, it was the realization Kelly's murder had set off such an uncomfortable chain of events. Neither Theo nor Mori felt safe at home, and if it hadn't been for Theo demanding to stay elsewhere, Damien wouldn't be dealing with the bombshell that his parents had owned a secret house that was warded against supernatural creatures.

I slept fitfully until my alarm went off about ten minutes before sunrise. Mori had pulled a thick flannel blanket out of the closet—it had been there when I moved in and smelled musty—and she rolled herself up in it before lying down on my bed. Even if the sun found a way through the aluminum foil I had taped to the windows, Mori would be safe from it since she was a vampire burrito.

I curled up on the love seat and tried to go back to sleep. I was finally dozing when I woke to the sensation of pins and needles shooting through my right foot. I couldn't see much in the dark, so I reached down to feel Felipe sitting on top of my foot, which had gone to sleep. I gently shook him off and sat up, flexing my toes to get the blood flowing.

My apartment felt like a cave. Even though the sun was up, no sunlight was getting past the aluminum foil covering my windows. I heard a sound to my left, and I turned on the lamp to see Felipe had climbed off the love seat and was at the door, scratching at the wood and looking at me anxiously.

I quickly changed into shorts and a T-shirt, then

grabbed the purple leash. Felipe resisted letting me put it around his neck until I said, "We don't go out until you have this on." I didn't know if he understood my words, or if he just decided he was tired of resisting. Either way, we were soon on our way down the steps and into the motel parking lot.

Thank goodness it was early. We didn't see a soul on our short walk, which meant I didn't have to lie to anyone about what Felipe was.

By eleven o'clock, I was downright antsy. I didn't want to do anything loud that might disturb Mori, and I was tired of sitting in a sunless apartment. Also, I had come up with an idea that I wanted to run by Damien. I showered as quietly as I could, refilled Felipe's water bowl, and drove to the Sanctuary.

When I arrived, there was no one to be seen. I wasn't surprised, since most of the Sanctuary's residents were nocturnal. I tugged on both of the front doors, but neither one would budge. Frustrated, I jiggled the latch on one of the doors while I pulled on the handle.

"Are you breaking into my haunt?" Damien's voice came from behind me, and I turned to see him standing there with his arms crossed. He was wearing his mirrored sunglasses, so I couldn't see enough of his face to know if he was amused or annoyed.

But it was Damien, so he was probably annoyed.

"It's not your haunt," I retorted. "And I'm not breaking in."

"It sure looks like it. Why are you here?"

Isn't he being direct this morning. I crossed my arms, too, mirroring Damien's stance. "As a matter of fact, I came here to talk to you."

Damien gestured toward me. "Talk away."

"I thought we could do this in your office," I suggested.

"I'm tired of being cooped up in there. It's why I just got back from a drive."

I could relate to that, so I began, "I know Justine and I insisted on bringing Allie and Jon here, but even Mori feels too uncomfortable to stay under the same roof with them, and not because she's afraid a slayer is on their tail."

Damien didn't look at all surprised by that, and I continued, "Just in case one of them is involved in this murder, I think we should be keeping an eye on them. And by 'we,' I mean Tanner and McCrory."

"Good idea," Damien said immediately. "I should have thought of that already. The ghosts can let us know if they see or hear anything of note from those two. Let's go have a chat with them."

Damien walked past me and had just pulled out his keys to unlock the front doors when one of them burst open. Madge, one of the three witches at the Sanctuary, stood in front of us. There was a panicked expression on her beautiful face, and her golden curls were tangled.

"I was asleep," she said breathlessly, "but I woke up when I felt your presence in my dreams." I wasn't sure if Madge was talking to me or to Damien, but I didn't have time to ask before she added, "You know I can tell when someone is lying, and there's an aura of falsehood coming from the room Allie and Jon are sharing."

CHAPTER TEN

Damien turned to me, and I saw one eyebrow rise above the top of his sunglasses. I hadn't known Damien for long, but I already recognized his *I told you so* look.

"Can you tell us anything more, Madge?" I asked.

She shook her head. "No. I started feeling it as soon as they arrived here, but the longer they're here, the more I'm able to tap into it. One of them, or maybe even both of them, is being deceitful. I don't know how or why, but I think we need to be cautious."

"Olivia and I are working on that," Damien assured Madge. "Tanner and McCrory are about to get an assignment."

Madge gave a short laugh. "Ghost spies? What a great idea."

Two forms appeared in the doorway behind Madge. Maida and Morgan stepped out, blinking in the daylight even though we were under the portico. Maida was wearing a long white nightdress, her two dark braids hanging over it. Morgan was wearing what looked like an old-fashioned bathrobe, and it had big black ruffles that partly obscured her wrinkled face.

"Have you delivered your message?" Maida asked in her high, childish voice. She looked to be only about ten years old, though with these three witches, there was no telling how old any of them really were.

"I have," said Madge.

"Perhaps you can sleep peacefully now that you're sharing the burden of knowledge," Morgan said.

Maida's face was grim. "It will be a burden for all of us to bear."

"We have each other," Morgan said confidently.

"And together, we can face the daylight," Madge and Maida chorused. It was something I had heard once before, when I was still new at my job. It seemed to be some kind of motto or mantra for the Sanctuary.

The three witches wished Damien and me a good morning, then glided back inside. I reached out and caught the door just before it closed behind them. The witches went up the grand staircase on the left-hand side of the entryway, but Damien and I headed to our right, down a hallway that led to his office.

Damien's office was a cozy place. The dark wood paneling and built-in bookshelves, combined with a massive desk and the overstuffed oxblood leather chairs, gave it a feeling of warmth while also lending the place an air of mystery. I liked the office itself, and I regretted that so little of the time I spent inside it was pleasant.

I shut the door to the office to make sure we had as much privacy as possible while Damien walked to a panel on the wall behind the desk. It looked vaguely like an electrical panel, but instead of switches for fuses, there were two columns of brass buttons, each with a handwritten label next to it.

Damien pressed one of the buttons, but nothing happened. I was just about to ask him what he was doing when I felt icy air waft across the back of my neck. I turned to see Connor McCrory looming behind me in his black trench coat and cowboy hat. His bushy mustache shimmered.

"Good morning, Mr. Shackleford. Ma'am." McCrory tipped his hat to me, and I smiled at the ghost.

"Where's Tanner?" Damien asked.

"Right behind you."

Damien whirled around just as Butch Tanner's form emerged from the wall. "I hate it when you do that," Damien muttered.

"Miss Olivia thinks it's funny," Tanner said. He pulled down the red bandana he always wore over his mouth and nose to give me a big grin. He was right: I was thoroughly amused by Damien's reaction.

"I'm sure she does." Damien motioned for Tanner to move in front of the desk, then said, "Olivia and I would like your help keeping an eye on our new guests."

McCrory crossed his arms. "Do you have reason to believe they might be guilty of a crime?"

"Madge says there's an aura of deception coming from their room, though she's not sure if it's from Allie, Jon, or both of them," I explained.

"In that case, I'm happy to help. I wouldn't want anyone doing something unlawful around here," McCrory said.

"Personally," Tanner broke in, "I think it would be nice if someone broke the rules for a change. But, since it's you asking, Miss Olivia, I'll do it."

Tanner and McCrory disappeared a few seconds later, going right through the door of Damien's office. Once they were gone, Damien said, "It would be a lot easier if we could just ask our guests if they're guilty."

I had been staring at the door, still not used to the fact I had ghosts for co-workers, and I turned to look at Damien thoughtfully. "Why can't we? I'm sure Allie and Jon can sense that everyone is a little wary of them, so they wouldn't be surprised if we asked them point-blank about their involvement in the murder."

"It might offend them," Damien pointed out.

"Then we'll ask politely."

Damien thought for a moment, then nodded. "Okay. But not until after the haunt closes tonight. I don't want any drama disrupting things."

I agreed, and since there wasn't much else to say, I drove back to my apartment. My plan was to grab my laptop and head up to the motel office so I could work in a place that had some daylight coming through the windows. When I walked in my front door, though, I realized I was going to have to put that plan on hold.

My refrigerator door was standing wide open, the bright light inside illuminating the floor in front of it, where a shredded Styrofoam tray still had a few bits of ground beef on it. The rest of the meat was gone, as was the plastic wrap that had been covering it. The cardboard box I had used to haul up a few yard sale finds didn't exist anymore, either. It had been ripped apart, and there were strips of cardboard littering my floor.

I looked around to find Felipe sitting on the love seat, little brown bits of cardboard stuck to his muzzle.

I wasn't all that upset about the ground beef. In fact, I was more impressed Felipe could open a fridge on his own. The cardboard, on the other hand, was something I would be picking out of my shag carpet until the day I moved out. Whenever that would be.

I closed the fridge, turned on a lamp, and cleaned up the mess as quietly as I could, until only tiny bits of cardboard were left. I would wait and vacuum those up after Mori got up at sundown. By the time I was finished, I was in no mood to sit down in front of my laptop. Instead, I wanted to get outside.

On my way out the door, I whispered a plea to Felipe

that he wouldn't wreck anything. *If I really do have any conjuring skills,* I thought, *then this is the time I really, really want them to work. I wish for Felipe to behave himself!*

I started walking toward the road with no clear idea of where I was going. I turned left and walked up Nightmare's main road for a bit, then made a right. High Noon Boulevard was ahead of me, and I was planning to walk right past it. As soon as the concrete sidewalk under my feet turned into wooden boards, though, I knew I wanted to go to the saloon. I turned and walked along High Noon Boulevard with a feeling of purpose.

The memorial to Kelly had grown, and two of the candles still burned. Inside, the saloon was only about half full. It wasn't quite time for lunch, though I did spy a few tourists drinking beer at the long bar across the back wall, despite the hour.

I hopped up onto a stool at the bar, and when the bartender came over, she smiled at me. "What'll ya have?" she asked.

"Actually, I'm looking for Frankie."

The bartender looked surprised, but she jabbed her thumb over her shoulder. "He's in his office. Go down the hallway toward the bathrooms and take the door on your left that says *Staff Only.*"

I thanked her and headed in that direction, but I paused in the hallway to think about what I was going to say. After my incredibly awkward conversation with Kelly's boyfriend, I was anxious to come off sounding less eccentric.

In the end, I decided to go for the direct approach. I went through the staff door and found myself in a short, dim hallway lined with enlarged black-and-white photos of what the saloon had looked like decades ago. The first door I came to was open, and a man was sitting at a desk inside it. I knocked lightly against the doorframe. "Excuse me, are you Frankie?"

The man glanced up, his eyes bloodshot behind his thick black-framed glasses. His brown hair was shaggy, and his T-shirt looked slightly askew, like he had been tugging on it. "Yeah," he said in a harried tone. "What do you need?"

I introduced myself, then dove right in with, "Is it true Kelly Lowry was stealing from the saloon?"

Frankie had only been giving me half of his attention, one hand still poised over the keyboard of his laptop. As soon as I said that, though, he looked at me sharply. "What's it to you?"

It was a fair question. I didn't want to lie, so I told him the first plausible truth that came to mind, since "I'm trying to determine whether this was the work of a vampire slayer" wouldn't cut it. "I helped Allie and her manager find a place to stay while they wait for this investigation to wrap up. The housing situation has become a bit tense, and the sooner they're on their way, the better. I trust the Nightmare Police Department to be thorough, but I figured it wouldn't hurt to do my own digging."

Frankie sneered at me. "I've already told the police about Kelly's past here, so I don't need to repeat it to you. Like you just said, we all trust them to be thorough, so I'm not going to answer questions from another snoop."

Another one? I wondered how many other interested locals had already come knocking at Frankie's door. I could tell by the set of his mouth I wasn't going to get anywhere with him, so I nodded sympathetically. "I'm sure you've been inundated by well-meaning people. I'll leave you alone."

Frankie pushed his glasses up on his nose and returned his attention to his laptop, acting like I wasn't even there anymore. In turn, I channeled my inner Damien: I left without another word.

I nearly ran into someone when I went through the staff door. I stopped short and apologized, and the woman stepped back to let me through. "No problem," she said. "Oh. You were here Monday night. You went backstage after Kelly..."

The woman, who looked like she was in her midtwenties, was dressed in the same type of saloon girl outfit Kelly had been. Her off-the-shoulder white blouse was low cut, disappearing under a tight red corset, and her ruffled black skirt was pinned up in the front to show off her fishnet stockings. I took a closer look at the woman's round cheeks and her brown hair, which cascaded in waves over her bare shoulders. "I remember you," I said. "I overheard you saying"—I looked behind me to make sure the staff door was closed, so there was no way Frankie would overhear us—"Kelly had been stealing from the saloon."

"Oh, yeah," the woman said. "It's no secret. Kelly stole from the tip jar and the cash register. But that's not the worst. She didn't just steal money. She stole my boyfriend, too!"

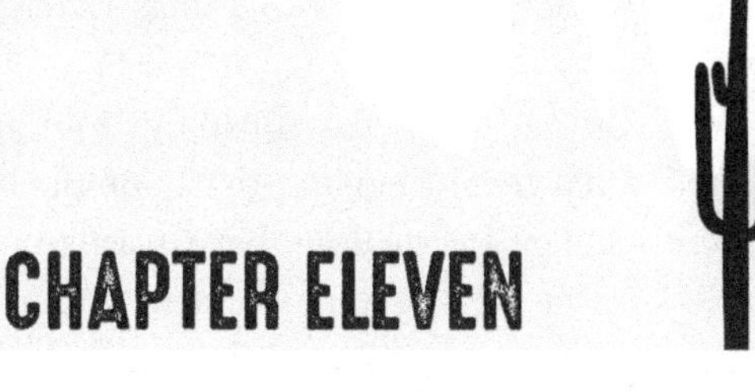

CHAPTER ELEVEN

"I'm sorry to hear it," I said. I meant it, too. Before I had gotten married to Mark, I hadn't really liked dating. There seemed to be as much heartbreak and bad dates as there were wonderful evenings and nice men. Now that I was divorced, every time I considered dating again, I would practically gag. It wasn't a game I wanted to get back into anytime soon, if ever. "I'm Olivia, by the way. My friend and I went backstage because Allie is the friend of a friend, and we wanted to check on her."

The woman gave me a little smile. "Tara Stokes. Nice to meet you."

"How long did you and Miguel date?" I asked.

"Two months and three days. Then Kelly just stole him right out from under me, like what Miguel and I had wasn't special."

For as big of a grudge as Tara seemed to be carrying, I had expected her answer to be a lot longer than two months and three days. Still, I put on my best "men are awful" face—which for me was fairly easy, considering I never would have broken down in Nightmare if it hadn't been for my ex—and said, "I'm so sorry. Is that around the time she was stealing from the saloon, too? Frankie wouldn't give me any details."

Tara shrugged. "Miguel and I dated almost a year ago,

but Kelly wasn't caught stealing until, oh, it was right at the end of tourist season." I must have looked confused, because Tara clarified, "The busy season for tourists is during the cooler months, so things quiet down around May."

So Kelly had been caught about four months before she died. That meant her murder hadn't been spur-of-the-moment revenge for stealing, but I wasn't crossing Frankie off the suspect list just yet. For that matter, I was adding Tara's name right underneath his on my mental list. She had a good motive, too.

"That means Kelly was stealing money from the saloon during the most lucrative time," I said. I had arrived in Nightmare in the middle of summer, and I expected tourist numbers would begin increasing again now that the weather was, allegedly, cooling off.

"She was literally caught with her hand in the cookie jar," Tara said. I could detect a hint of glee in her tone. "Seriously: we use an old cookie jar to hold the cash tips."

"Why didn't Frankie fire her?" I asked. It's what I would have done.

Tara shrugged. "We were flooded with tourists at the time, and we were short-staffed. He needed her, and apparently, they worked out a deal for her to pay him back, though none of us were repaid for the missing tip money." Tara pursed her lips and threw a judgmental look over my shoulder, in the direction of Frankie's office. "The problem is, there's no way of knowing exactly how much Kelly stole, or for how long she had been doing it. I'm sure she lied about how much she had taken."

I nodded. Tara seemed to be on a roll, and I didn't want to say anything that might slow her down. She continued, "You know what the worst part is? She claimed she was taking the money and saving it up so she could get out of this town. She had some idea about eloping with

Miguel. She was stealing tip money that I should have gotten a share of, all so she could run off and marry the guy she stole from me!"

Tara gasped and clapped a hand over her mouth. She looked at me with wide eyes, and I knew exactly what she was thinking: she had just made it sound like she should be suspect number one in Kelly's murder.

"Anyway," Tara said in a rush as she lowered her hand, "Kelly seemed more upset about not getting the free money anymore than she did about getting caught. She whined all the time about how she needed cash. Maybe she was really serious about leaving Nightmare. Who knows? I've got to get to work. Um, it was nice meeting you." Tara flashed a smile, and I took it as her attempt to get on my good side, so I wouldn't linger on her motives for murder.

I left the saloon, feeling gratified that I had been able to get some answers, and that those answers seemed to point to Kelly's murder having absolutely nothing to do with Allie or Jon. And, certainly, nothing to do with a vampire slayer. I still didn't know why Kelly had been so jittery during her last haircut with Mia, but it was looking more and more like her murder had to do with something that had happened long before Allie or Jon arrived in Nightmare. Kelly could have been killed by an angry employer she stole from, a bitter co-worker who lost a boyfriend to her, her own boyfriend, or some other local who had an issue with her.

As I walked slowly down High Noon Boulevard, I reminded myself that if this murder didn't involve anything related to the supernatural or someone I was friends with, then it didn't need to involve me, either. It wasn't my business, and I should stay out of it.

Unfortunately, my walk took me right past The Neon Coyote. The giant plaster coyote out front was a fluorescent shade of yellow that was hard to look at in broad daylight. At the same time, though, it felt like a kind of beacon, beckoning me toward the biker bar it sat in front of.

My feet were moving toward it even while my mind was saying this murder was none of my business. It was like I couldn't help it. I wanted to know without a shred of doubt this was nothing but a normal murder—if there even was such a thing—so Mori and Theo could move back into the Sanctuary, and we could all get on with our lives without worrying about someone lurking around town with a wooden stake.

The Neon Coyote was in a low adobe building that had no windows. The front door was dark wood with a metal latticework over it. It looked more like the entrance to a medieval castle in England than a biker bar in Arizona. I tugged it open and walked inside.

There were only about five patrons sitting at the bar, which formed a big square in the middle of the room. To my right were three pool tables. It was dark and smoky inside, and I resisted the urge to pinch my nose to block the smell of cigarettes.

You know in movies, where someone walks into a place they shouldn't be, and whatever music is playing immediately stops with a piercing scratch as everyone turns to stare? That's just about what happened when I walked into The Neon Coyote. It was my own record scratch moment. The heavy rock music coming from the jukebox didn't stop, but almost as one, everyone in the place put down their drinks or stood up from the shots they were about to take at the pool table to stare at me.

To be fair, it was glaringly obvious I didn't fit in there. The only other woman was behind the bar, and she was wearing about seventy-five percent less clothing than I was. My own outfit was another dead giveaway that I had wandered into a place I didn't belong: my white T-shirt and olive-green shorts made me look like I should be on my way to the grocery store in an SUV, not walking into a biker bar. I was pretty sure The Neon Coyote had the highest concentration of studded black leather in the entire town of Nightmare. How did these guys dress like this without sweating to death?

I felt horribly awkward, especially when I noticed Miguel was one of the men standing at a pool table. While the others looked anywhere from unwelcoming to simply curious, Miguel had a look of dismay on his face. Was it because I had caught him holding a pool cue, much like the one that had recently been used to stab his girlfriend? Or was it because he didn't want another strange conversation with me?

It was definitely the latter. As I got closer to him, Miguel slowly backed up. He put one end of his pool cue on the floor in front of him, his grip on it so tight his knuckles were white. "Look, lady," he said nervously, "I don't want any trouble."

I did what was probably the wrong thing in that moment, but I couldn't help it. I laughed. Here I was, a middle-aged woman in a biker bar full of men twice my size, and one of the bikers was telling me he didn't want any trouble. I really had made a bad impression on Miguel.

My laughter only made Miguel look more nervous, and I immediately stopped when two of the men near him stepped forward. "Sorry," I said. "Miguel, I know I said some strange things last night after the vigil. I guess I'm having a hard time shaking the idea that whoever killed Kelly has watched one too many vampire movies."

Miguel's grip on the pool cue loosened. "I know what you mean. We've all been saying the same thing."

"May I please ask you something?" I began, but

Miguel's friends took another step closer to me before I could continue.

Miguel held out a hand. "It's okay, guys. This is the woman who got Ella from The Lusty out of jail. She might be able to help us."

So Miguel had asked around about me after we had met. That was a bit unsettling, but not surprising. In a town as small as Nightmare, everyone seemed to know everyone else. Since I was a stranger to Miguel, he had probably put my name on his own suspect list until he'd had a chance to find out who I was and why I was rambling about vampires at our first meeting.

"Come on," Miguel said, handing his pool cue to one of his friends. He led me to a round high-top table in a far corner of the bar. Once we were seated, he asked, "You want a shot?"

I shook my head. "Oh, no, thank you. I only came in hoping you'd be here."

"Your questions about vampires the other night… That was strange, but then I found out you work at Nightmare Sanctuary. You sort of live in a horror movie, so of course, you thought of vampires with the way Kelly was killed."

When Miguel said "horror movie," I didn't know if he was referring to the fact I worked in a place that made guests feel like they were immersed in a horror movie, or if he was referring to my co-workers. Plenty of Nightmare's normal residents thought everyone who worked at the Sanctuary was weird and possibly dangerous.

To their credit, they were right about the dangerous part. I wouldn't want to get on the bad side of a vampire or a banshee.

I tried to look abashed, like Miguel had correctly pegged me as a haunted house employee with an overactive imagination. "Believe it or not, the reason I'm here is because of something you said about vampires. I overheard you say Allie—the singer who was supposed to be performing on Monday—was a soul-sucking vampire. What did you mean by that?"

"She's staying at the haunted house, isn't she?" Miguel asked snidely. "You should ask her. When she was here a year ago, she was horrible to Kelly. Plus, there was the body."

CHAPTER TWELVE

My mouth dropped open. "What body?" I asked slowly.

"Don't you remember? It was on the front page of the newspaper for at least a week."

"I'm new in Nightmare, remember? I haven't even been here for two months."

"Right, that's right. Well, Allie came through here about this time last year, and the next morning, someone found a body behind the saloon. She was still wearing her saloon girl outfit, just like Kelly was." Miguel's voice broke when he said his girlfriend's name, and he turned away from me so I could only see a sliver of his face. "By then," he continued, still facing the wall rather than me, "Allie was long gone, and the police had to track her down so they could question her. She swore she was innocent, and that she packed up and left right after the show."

Maybe Theo and Mori were right to move out of the Sanctuary as long as Allie is in it. Even though I knew there was a chance Allie and Jon were involved in Kelly's murder, I had figured it was a long shot. It had seemed more likely they weren't involved at all, or, at worst, that Allie herself was being targeted by a slayer or some other enemy who wanted to send a message. Instead, it was looking like Allie might have already committed murder in Nightmare once, and she had just done it again. A dead body turning up at the saloon on each of her visits seemed like too much of a coincidence.

I sighed. Here I had convinced myself this murder wasn't anything for me to stick my nose into. But, if my friends at the Sanctuary were possibly sharing a roof with a killer, then I needed to find out for sure.

"And you said Allie was horrible to Kelly," I said. "Horrible how?"

Miguel finally faced me again, and by the way one side of his mouth was twitching, I knew he was fighting to hold it together. When he started talking, though, I could hear the anger outweighing his grief. "She treated Kelly like trash. She was really demanding, and nothing Kelly did was good enough for Allie. She yelled at her and called her incompetent."

That didn't sound at all like the Allie I had met, who seemed to be fairly even-tempered, even when someone had been staked just a few feet away from her. Those who had met her when she was in Nightmare the last time spoke positively of her, and I knew they wouldn't be so upbeat about a total diva.

"So you can see," Miguel said ominously, "why I'm a little upset that the freaks at the haunted house are letting her stay there. She's a murderer and a horrible person. Plus, she's just weird."

"Weird how?" I asked. Miguel clearly thought poorly about those of us who worked at the Sanctuary, so Allie must have behaved very oddly if he felt she was even stranger than the rest of us.

"She refused to come out of her van until two hours before the show, like a celebrity who won't mingle with everyone else. Her manager was really particular about her schedule, saying Allie wouldn't come inside the saloon until a certain time, because she needed to rest her voice and her body. Once it was dark out, she emerged like some kind of diva." Miguel sneered, but I suspected Allie's late appearance was because she had been in her van, sleeping until sundown. It had nothing to do with her thinking she was too good for everyone.

"And then there was the water," Miguel continued. When I cocked an eyebrow, he leaned forward, like he was sharing a big secret with me. "Performers at the saloon get paid, but they also get a bar tab for food and drinks. Allie asked for extra cash instead of a tab. It's not too strange—some musicians need every penny they can get—except Allie claimed it was because she was on a special diet and couldn't eat the food they serve at the saloon. Kelly took a pitcher of ice water to the dressing room, but Allie never even touched it. She's a singer, and you'd think she would go through a ton of water. She didn't eat or drink a single thing that night. Even the saloon's water wasn't good enough for her and her *diet*?" Miguel laughed sardonically.

I managed to respond with a small laugh of my own, but Miguel's words were a bit frightening. He had recognized the signs of Allie being a vampire without even making the connection. If he took those clues along with my comments about vampires, he might become a believer quickly. I consoled myself that, at any rate, Miguel was clearly not a vampire slayer himself.

"Did you ever meet Allie?" I asked.

Miguel nodded. "Yeah. Kelly had told me how horrible she was last year. So, this time, I went to the saloon to make sure she treated Kelly with respect. I was here at the bar beforehand, and I grabbed a pool cue to take with me. I wasn't going to hurt her with it, but I figured I could threaten her if I needed to. But then I met her, and she was acting like a decent human being, so I put the pool cue in a corner backstage."

If Miguel was telling the truth, then that explained why a pool cue had been present the night of the murder. That just left me wondering who had snapped it in half and used it as a weapon. "You don't know who took it?" I asked.

Miguel's face tightened, and his mouth twitched again. "No. At first, I didn't even realize it had been used to… If I hadn't shown up with it that night, then maybe she would still be alive. What if her death is my fault?"

"If the pool cue hadn't been there, the killer would have found another way," I said sympathetically. "You can't blame yourself." *Unless, of course,* I added silently, *you are the killer.* I wasn't taking Miguel off my list just yet.

Miguel sniffed loudly. "You're right."

There didn't seem to be anything else to say, and Felipe would probably be ready for another walk soon, so I thanked Miguel and left. I was glad to know how the pool cue had wound up at the crime scene, but it was probably information the police already had. I wasn't breaking any new ground. And, of course, the police would know all about the murder the year before. What they didn't know was that Allie was a vampire who needed human blood to survive.

I was brooding when Mori woke up at sundown and found me sitting on the love seat, my knees pulled up under my chin and my arms wrapped around my shins. Brooding was her word, not mine. It was the first thing Mori said when she unwrapped herself from the blanket, and I begrudgingly told her about the death the year before. I didn't want her to feel any more uncomfortable around Allie and Jon than she already did.

Mori surprised me, though, by saying, "We all heard about that. Guests who came to the Sanctuary that night were buzzing with the news, but I don't think Allie would kill her dinner, then dump the body right there where she was playing."

Mori made a good point, and I felt slightly better as we drove over to the Sanctuary for work that night.

Every evening at Nightmare Sanctuary Haunted House began with what I thought of as a family meeting. Justine would fill us in with the latest news and announcements, then dole out assignments for those of us who tended to float from one job to another.

I settled onto a bench at one of the tables in the massive dining room just as Malcolm sat down opposite me. He leaned forward and wrapped his long, spindly fingers around my wrist. "Are you doing okay?" he asked.

"Me? Yeah, I'm okay. Why?" I actually glanced down at my black Sanctuary T-shirt and jeans, like I might find evidence there of my not-okayness.

"You haven't looked this nervous since your very first night with us."

"Why are you nervous?" The voice that piped up right next to me was Theo's. He had sat down without me even noticing, as usual. If I ever needed someone to do clandestine work for me, Theo would be my go-to guy.

"I'm not nervous," I protested.

Mori, who was sitting on my other side, made a noise of disbelief. Quietly, she said, "Olivia learned about the murder that happened the last time Allie was in town. She's worried she brought the fox into the chicken coop."

Theo was already in his zombie pirate costume, so his look of scrutiny was extra creepy. "Surely not," he said. "I don't think Allie did that. She knows how careful we all have to be in our communities so we don't draw unwanted attention." Theo glanced toward a table at the front of the dining room, just in front of the small platform Justine was walking across. I saw Allie and Jon sitting there, looking as nervous as I felt.

Justine stepped up to the podium and called us all to attention with a hearty, "Good evening!" After mentioning a few items, like an out-of-order toilet, she got to assignments for the night. I would be at the front, taking tickets from our guests.

After I'd heard that, I stopped paying attention, but my ears perked up when Justine said, "And you all know Allie and Jon by now. They'll be lending a hand tonight, as well. Allie will join Mori in the mausoleum corridor, and Jon will be in the hospital vignette."

I glanced to my right, but Mori's expression was placid. As soon as Justine finished up, I whispered, "Did you know you were getting a teammate tonight?"

"No, but it's okay. Remember, Allie isn't the one who makes me nervous."

Right. I had forgotten Mori's hang-up was with Jon and his over-protective attitude toward Allie. Mori and I were both suspicious but of different people.

I wished everyone at my table a fun night of scaring guests, then slowly made my way to the entrance. Zach was already at his usual spot in the ticket window, which was in the alcove near the front doors. We didn't open for nearly half an hour, but there was already someone standing there with cash.

The first hour of the evening dragged past. Wednesdays weren't typically busy, anyway, and this seemed to be the slowest night I had experienced since I had started working at the Sanctuary. The stanchions and red velvet ropes in the entryway were pointless, since there was no line snaking back and forth. By nine o'clock, Justine had come by to rearrange the ropes so people could go straight from the front doors to the entry of the haunt.

During one long break between guests, I dashed over to the ticket window to talk to Zach. Before I could say anything, though, he looked over my shoulder. "You're up," he said.

I looked back and saw Malcolm, who touched a hand

to his top hat and waved me over. It was time for my break, and he was there to relieve me. "Get ready for boredom," I warned him as I scooted through the doors.

As soon as I reached the dining room, I turned toward the snack table so I could grab a bag of chips, but I paused when I saw Allie. She was sitting by herself at one of the tables, sipping something inside a Styrofoam cup. There was a lid on the cup, but the straw was clear, and I could see the dark-red liquid moving upward.

My stomach lurched. It was one thing to think about vampires drinking blood, but it was another to see it with my own eyes. And, somehow, Allie sipping it so casually out of a cup seemed to make it worse.

However, it was the first time I had seen her without Jon hovering over her like a helicopter mom. This was my chance to have a private chat with her. I lightly pressed a hand over my stomach and silently commanded it to settle down, then walked over and sat on the bench across the table from Allie. "Hi," I said lightly. "How's the haunting going?"

Allie gave me a small smile. Her fangs weren't as long as Mori's, and it was easy to understand how she could tour the country without being recognized as a vampire. "It's not bad, but it's hard to get in the spirit given everything that's going on."

"Maybe it's good to have a distraction like this."

Allie put her cup down, and I had to avert my eyes. The end of the straw had a single red drop on it. "You know," she said frankly, "I didn't like that girl at all. Kelly was horrible to work with during my last tour, but I certainly didn't want her dead."

CHAPTER THIRTEEN

I frowned at Allie. "You thought Kelly was horrible to work with? She apparently said the same thing about you."

Allie laughed. "That sounds about right. If a venue gives me a bar tab, I always ask for cash instead. It's not like anyone has blood on tap! But Kelly seemed to take my request personally. She accused me of being cheap, saying I did it so I didn't have to tip her for bringing drinks to the dressing room. Then she brought me a pitcher of water and said I shouldn't be such a snob, and that the saloon had really good beer if I would just try it. She made snide comments to me all night long."

After what Tara had said about Kelly stealing Miguel away from her and taking money from the saloon, this scenario sounded more plausible than the one Miguel had presented. Kelly seemed to be someone who only looked out for herself. I wondered if Kelly had disliked Allie for some reason, then twisted the story of their interaction to garner sympathy from Miguel.

"I heard Kelly was acting nervous leading up to your show this week," I said. "I wonder if she worried you'd retaliate for her attitude the last time around."

"She definitely seemed worried. Not only was Kelly overly polite to me and Jon, but she was jumpy. I reached for my guitar, which happened to be near her, and she literally screeched, like I was trying to hurt her. Then, the last time I saw her that night, she talked to me in this really shaky voice, asking things like where else I toured and what life was like on the road. It felt forced, and she kept looking over her shoulder the whole time. Honestly, for a moment, I thought she had figured out what I am. She seemed that scared."

My thoughts went back to Mori's distrust of Jon. Had he threatened Kelly? Had Jon told Kelly that her previous behavior wouldn't be tolerated? Suddenly, I was beginning to think Mori was the one who was on the right track. It was even possible Kelly really had learned the truth about Allie, and Jon killed her to keep her silent. He was always watching Allie like a hawk, maybe because Allie wasn't good at hiding her vampiric nature. Even Miguel had seen all the signs.

"Olivia?" Allie asked. She was looking at me intently.

I cut off my meandering thoughts and took a deep breath. This was it: my chance to ask Allie about the first dead saloon girl. I didn't want to outright accuse her of murder, so I began, "Do you think it's possible—"

I cut off abruptly at the sound of the dining room door banging open. Jon ran through it, and he didn't stop until he was at our table. "There you are!" he nearly shouted at Allie. "I went to check on you, but you weren't there."

"I'm on break," Allie said, tapping a finger against her cup. "Mori should have told you."

"She did, but I shouldn't have had to ask her. You should have told me."

Allie turned to me. "Jon thinks I'll get myself into trouble if I don't have constant supervision," she said apologetically. "He's being even more vigilant while we wait to know if there's a vampire slayer in town."

"I don't think there is," I said honestly. "Kelly had

enemies that have nothing to do with the supernatural world. I'm pretty sure she was killed for revenge."

"Revenge?" Jon asked. He straightened his disheveled hospital gown, a costume splattered with fake blood.

"Kelly's boss and one of her co-workers both had motives. And believe me, it's nothing nearly as dramatic or interesting as a vampire slayer."

"That's good," Allie said. She lifted the cup and brought the straw to her lips. "Hopefully, the police will have this sorted in no time."

"Hopefully." I stood. My break wasn't over just yet, but I knew there was no way I would be able to eat my chips while Allie was sitting there with what I was thinking of as her vampire sippy cup. *Ew.* Instead, I wandered out into the hallway. The door at the end, which led to the entryway, was closed, so no guests would see me shoving chips into my mouth before I had to get back to my post.

I spent the rest of my night taking turns between greeting the trickle of guests handing me their tickets and pondering the strange dynamic between Allie and Jon. Even without factoring in the two murders, I was beginning to understand why Jon unnerved Mori. He seemed almost obsessed with Allie. I nearly laughed at the idea of a human following Mori around like that. She would give them the slip in under a minute, I was sure.

It was nearly midnight, which was closing time for the Sanctuary, when Malcolm came around again. I winked at him as I asked, "Do I get a second break tonight?"

Malcolm smiled. "No, I'm letting you know Allie is going to give a performance in the dining room at half after midnight. Since she didn't get to play at the saloon, she thought it would be nice to treat all of us."

It was nice, and I readily agreed. Not only was I interested in observing both her and Jon some more, but I was also eager to finally hear Allie play and sing.

The half hour between closing and showtime gave everyone who was in costume a chance to change back into their regular clothes. Of course, for people like Malcolm and the three witches, it wasn't necessary, since their costumes and their everyday clothes were one and the same.

Another Sanctuary resident who didn't need to change clothes was Seraphina, the siren, who got around in a small portable water tank. Fiona, a banshee with long black hair and pale skin, rolled Seraphina into the dining room right on my heels, so the three of us chatted while we waited for the show to start.

Seraphina brushed a wet lock of golden hair out of her face, her faintly green skin glowing under the overhead lights. "This is really great for me, since I can't go to the saloon. I was bummed on Monday, thinking I was missing out on the show."

"It was a show all right," I muttered.

Fiona laughed, a deep, musical sound. "And of course you've thrown yourself into the middle of it, Olivia. McCrory is going to have to make you an honorary deputy."

"No, thanks. I'm only interested in Kelly's murder until we determine that Allie isn't in danger, or that…"

I was hesitant to say the rest, but Seraphina nodded knowingly, sending a shower of waterdrops flying. "Or that we're not in danger from her," she finished.

I just smiled tightly in response. The sooner we got this murder solved, the sooner everyone at the Sanctuary could breathe a sigh of relief and relax.

We moved on to talking about the night and how slow it had been, until Allie stepped up onto the stage, her guitar in hand. Those of us who were still standing settled onto the benches at the tables, except for Seraphina, whose long silver tail confined her to her mobile tank.

"Good evening, friends," Allie said into the microphone. Someone turned off all but the overhead lights closest to the stage, and we quieted down. "I just want to say how much we appreciate your hospitality. I don't know what we would do if it weren't for your generosity in letting us be a part of your lives. This first song is about finding that special someone who makes you feel whole, and I'd like to dedicate it to all of you."

Allie strummed her guitar and began to sing. As the song progressed, I felt my eyelids droop. I blinked rapidly and shook my head. Vampires had the ability to mesmerize, and I wasn't sure if Allie was using it on her audience, or if I was just sleepy after an unbelievably long few days.

I also wondered if one of the perks of being a vampire was the ability to sing beautifully. Allie had a gorgeous voice, and when she thanked us and told us to have a good night, I glanced at my watch and was surprised she had already played for forty-five minutes. It hadn't seemed that long. I joined in the enthusiastic cheers and applause. While I did, I scanned the audience and saw Damien was there, leaning against the back wall. Despite the darkness of the room, he was wearing his mirrored sunglasses, and his expression was, as usual, impenetrable.

I turned to Fiona, Seraphina, and Gunnar, who had also joined us. "She's incredible," I said enthusiastically.

Fiona nodded. "Last year was her first time in Nightmare, and we all fell in love with her music. I'm so glad she came back."

"And Sera and I are glad she played here, so we could understand why the rest of you have been hyping her up for the past year," Gunnar said. "Zach said we're going to have an afterparty. Olivia, are you going to join us?"

Damien was already walking out of the dining room. He hadn't stopped to talk to a single person.

"Maybe in a bit," I told Gunnar distractedly. "I want to check on Damien first."

Fiona snorted. "What, are you checking to make sure he's not a robot under that human-looking exterior?"

"Don't be silly, Fi," Seraphina said with a grin. "She's checking his jerk level to make sure he hasn't accidentally become a nicer person."

I had always been happy to listen to the Damien bashing, or even to participate in it, regardless of Mama's admonition for me to go easy on him. In that moment, though, I suddenly felt a wave of sympathy for Damien. Yes, he was a standoffish jerk who treated everyone at the Sanctuary like they were beneath him. But he was also a man whose father was missing, whose absent mother was a mystery, and who didn't have any idea what he was or what he was capable of.

What a terrifying way to live, I thought. *I'd probably act like a jerk, too.*

Of course, I knew Damien wouldn't want me sharing any of those details, except the one everyone already knew about. "Maybe he's taking his dad's disappearance harder than we give him credit for," I suggested.

Gunnar clicked his teeth together, his fangs flashing menacingly. "You're going to make me feel sorry for him, if you're not careful."

I put my hand on Gunnar's broad bicep and gave it a squeeze. "I'm not worried about that happening anytime soon. I'll see you all in a bit."

Halfway to the door, Felipe ran up to me. He stood on his hind legs and wrapped his front paws around my thigh. I reached down and scratched his head until he let me go and darted toward the witches to get attention from them, too.

Damien had already disappeared down the hallway by the time I made it out of the dining room, but I was certain I would find him in his office, so I headed for the front hallway.

The office door was open, and I had almost reached it when I heard a voice that wasn't Damien's. I stopped walking and leaned slightly forward, listening.

Damien had just said something, and even though I didn't catch his words, I could hear the way the sentence ended in a questioning tone.

The first voice I had heard answered, and I realized it was Jon. "I don't know what we're going to do. We can't make money if she's not playing shows, and Allie needs to feed properly soon. She can't keep living like this."

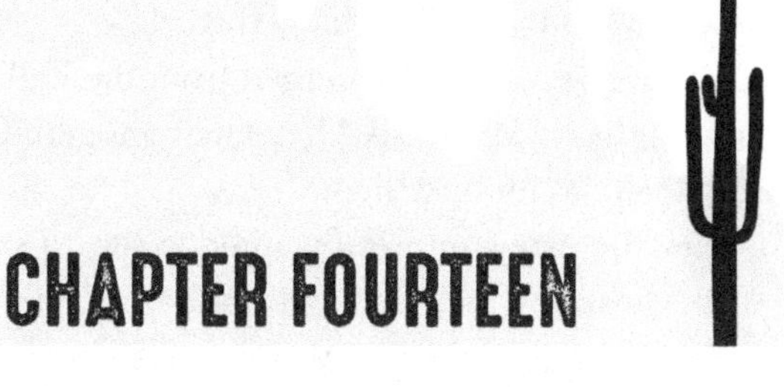

CHAPTER FOURTEEN

"I'm doing my best, Jon," Damien said. "You two are getting free room and board here, and I'm paying you to work the haunt, even though we don't need the extra help, and despite the fact it's hurting our budget. We're not a charity, but I'm doing what I can to help you."

"I know, I know, but this isn't sustainable," Jon answered, sounding piqued.

I began creeping backward as quietly as I could. The last thing I wanted was to be caught eavesdropping. What Jon had said made sense: the sooner the murder was wrapped up, the sooner he and Allie would be allowed to leave Nightmare and get back on tour. Without money from playing shows, they would be in danger of going broke.

Boy, could I relate to that. As someone who had so recently been broke, too, I understood Jon's sense of urgency.

I was slightly annoyed with both Jon's and Damien's ends of the conversation. While I admired Damien for giving Jon and Allie work, he was taking the martyr route, making it sound like the Sanctuary was going to suffer financially because of it. At the same time, Jon didn't sound all that grateful for the money.

The thing that seemed even more important than the

battle of the attitudes, though, was Jon's mention that Allie needed to "properly" feed. What did that even mean? If I asked either Jon or Damien about it, they would know their conversation had been overheard.

Luckily, as soon as I emerged from the hallway into the entryway, I saw Mori and Theo talking together. Felipe was running circles around them.

"Just the two vampires I wanted to see," I said.

"Because you miss my handsome face?" Theo asked.

"No, though you do look a lot more attractive without the zombie makeup." I stepped close to the two of them, threw a glance around the room to make sure we were alone, and said, "Are there vampires who have special diets? Like, can a vampire be allergic to Type O Positive, or something?"

Mori and Theo looked at each other, then they both shook their heads. "Not that I've ever heard of," Mori said.

"Everyone's blood tastes a little different, of course," said Theo. "I used to know a vampire who preferred drinking from people leaving a tavern in the wee hours of the morning. She swore she got a buzz from the alcohol in their system. But I've never heard of a vampire who had dietary restrictions."

"Huh. I wonder what my blood tastes like?"

I had meant the question more for myself, but Theo looked at me slyly. "I'll be happy to tell you."

"Yuck. No! I'm not a snack!"

"Speaking of snacks," Mori said, "Felipe and I are going out so I can get a bite. We'll return to your apartment late, but we promise to be quiet."

I assured Mori that was no problem, and I even wished her luck. I knew she would be looking for a tourist she could mesmerize, which meant she could send them on their way after she drank their blood, and they would have no memory of the event.

Mori and Felipe must have kept their promise to be quiet when they got back to my place, because I didn't stir until my alarm went off at dawn. I crawled out of bed and relocated to the love seat while Mori settled in for her own sleep. I drifted off again pretty quickly, but I woke up when I felt like pins were shooting through my cheek. It had been one thing for my foot to fall asleep on Tuesday night, but my face?

Except when I put a hand to my cheek, I could feel Felipe's paw. He wasn't scratching me, but his claws were extended, pressing just hard enough against my skin to get my attention. I fumbled for the lamp, and when it turned on, I could see Felipe staring at me intently. "What?" I asked him.

Felipe jumped down from the love seat and made a beeline for the door, then looked back at me anxiously. "Coming, coming," I told him groggily. I threw off my blanket, slid into my shoes, and grabbed his leash.

I was still half-asleep as I led Felipe down the stairs and to the alley that ran behind the motel. It wasn't until we were on our way back that I snapped fully awake. Mama was walking right toward us. She had a stack of white towels in her arms, and she tilted her chin up to gaze at Felipe over the top of them. "Olivia, good morning. I didn't know you had adopted a *dog*."

I could hear the sarcasm on that last word. Mori had told me I could pass Felipe off as a hairless greyhound, but there was no way I could lie to Mama. I also couldn't tell her the absolute truth, so I said, "I have a friend staying with me for a few nights. Felipe belongs to her."

"Mm-hm," Mama said, her eyes narrowed at Felipe. After a few seconds, she looked up at me. "The funeral is today, and I expect it's going to be the social event of the month. Want to go?"

Do I? I hadn't known Kelly, so there was really no reason I should be there.

Mama must have sensed my hesitation, because she added, "Since you like tracking down murderers, this could be a good chance for you to observe suspects."

"You know me so well," I admitted.

"We'll leave here at three thirty. I'll drive." Mama spared one last glance at Felipe, then continued on her way.

"That was close, Felipe," I whispered as I walked him up the stairs to my door. He didn't answer, of course. He just wagged his tail.

I felt like I was getting little clues that could be a big help, but I was hitting dead ends when it came to pursuing them. Allie had some kind of special diet, but if I asked her about it, I would have to admit I had been eavesdropping on her manager. Kelly had been talking to Mia and Allie about leaving town, all while acting nervous, but I couldn't exactly press Kelly for more details.

I did consider her ghost might still be around, and perhaps Tanner and McCrory could track her down for a quick interview, but that seemed like a long shot.

Instead, I headed to the Nightmare Public Library after I had showered and had my morning coffee. I wanted more details about the woman who had been murdered a year before.

The library was just off High Noon Boulevard, down on the south end of the street. I drove instead of making the ten-minute walk. Even though the weather was cooler than it had been just a couple of weeks before, it was far from what I considered fall weather, and I just didn't feel like getting sweaty so early in the morning.

When I asked the librarian where I could find past issues of *The Nightmare Journal*, she pointed over my shoulder. "Across the street. The newspaper office keeps all those on file."

"You don't have any here?" I asked pleadingly. The idea of walking into the newspaper office filled me with dread. I had only been there once, and during the visit, I had realized one of the reporters was a murderer and proceeded to chase him down the stairs. Not only would going back there bring the feelings of that day into sharp focus, but it would be slightly embarrassing, too. I was sure my confrontation with Ross Banning had left quite an impression on the rest of the newspaper staff.

After the librarian informed me she only had that day's copy of *The Nightmare Journal*, I thanked her and walked across the street. I could feel a slight shake in my hands as I reached out and grasped the handle of the newspaper office's front door. When I got inside, though, only one person spared me a glance, and that was the man sitting behind the counter right in front of me. "Hello, classified ads can be placed upstairs. You'll see the sign once you're up there." He waved in the direction of the staircase, his eyes already back on the newspaper in his other hand.

"I'm here to look through your archives," I told him.

The man waved me in the same direction without looking at me again. "Downstairs. Put away whatever you take out. No one here wants to clean up a mess."

In any other situation, I would have been annoyed by the man's dismissive attitude. However, in this case, I decided inattention was preferable to decent customer service. I had been greeted by the same man on my previous visit to *The Nightmare Journal*'s office, and I was glad he wasn't paying enough attention to realize I was the one who had caused such a ruckus over Ross Banning.

The open space behind the front counter was full of desks, and although there were more people sitting at them than I had seen the last time, the room was still far from crowded. Apparently, when the building had been erected in the late eighteen hundreds, there had been a lot more news to report in Nightmare, and a lot more journalists on staff to cover it all.

There was a slight musty smell on the ground floor, and it only grew stronger as I descended the stairs into the basement. I opened the door at the bottom and fumbled for a light switch on the wall. During the few seconds it took my fingers to find it, I imagined all kinds of scary things in the darkness of the room before me.

Then the harsh, fluorescent lights overhead blared to life, and I squinted at rows of tall wooden shelves, all holding plastic boxes stuffed with issues of the newspaper. It wasn't a fancy filing system, but it would do.

I walked straight down the row just in front of me, but the boxes were labeled with dates, which quickly told me I was sixty years too early. I headed to a different row, whose shelves were half empty, and easily found the boxes labeled with the previous year.

If Allie had been in Nightmare around the same time the year before, then that meant I could start with issues from September. I hefted a box labeled *August 27-September 19* off the shelf and carried it over to a small table against one wall.

Miguel had mentioned the saloon girl's murder had been all over the front page of the newspaper, and it didn't take me long to find what I was looking for. The issue for Monday, September 17, had a headline in capital letters: *MURDER AT THE SALOON.*

I sat down in a rickety metal folding chair and began to read. The story said a woman named Sarah Alton, just twenty-two years old, had been found in the alley behind the saloon.

The article went on to say there were marks on the ground that indicated Sarah had dragged herself from behind a dumpster on one side of the alley to the saloon on the opposite side, making it all the way to the backstage door, where she expired.

I shuddered. That meant she hadn't been dead yet when her killer had left the scene. "Poor girl," I said quietly.

It was a sentence buried in the middle of a paragraph that really got my attention, though. The writer casually mentioned that when the police searched Sarah's body, they had found something in the pocket of her frilly, old-fashioned skirt: a CD autographed to her from Allie.

CHAPTER FIFTEEN

I realized the autographed CD on the victim's body looked bad for Allie, and the author of the article hinted at the same thing. Allie had already left Nightmare by the time Sarah's body was found, so the police hadn't yet been able to question her or her manager at the time the article was written.

Once I finished reading, I put the newspaper down with a sigh. I kept hoping to absolutely rule out Allie and Jon as suspects or targets, but I kept veering toward confirming them as suspects. The fact Sarah had been so close to where Allie had been playing definitely seemed suspicious, and it was easy to understand why the police were keen to keep her in town until the current murder had been solved.

I flipped through the following week of newspapers, but they didn't disclose much. The police did finally have a phone interview with Allie, but they hadn't been able to pin anything on her. Officers in charge of the case seemed to have pretty quickly hit a dead end, so future articles were mostly a rehash of the original one, with plenty of speculation and promises to report additional details as soon as they came to light. Six days after the first mention of the murder, the newspaper headline was about a rodeo being held in a nearby town. The Nightmare news cycle had moved on.

The original article did give me one detail I hadn't had before: Sarah had bled to death due to a small cut on her neck. I realized it could have been the work of a vampire's fangs, but Allie just didn't strike me as a killer. Neither did Jon, for that matter. For all of his obsessive, over-protective behavior, there was still an air of timidity about him. I wondered if Allie and Sarah had gotten in a fight, and the death was accidental. Did vampires get bitey when they were angry? I'd have to ask Mori and Theo.

I dutifully repacked the newspapers into the plastic box and returned it to its rightful spot on the shelf. I trudged up the stairs, disappointed I hadn't learned anything that would help clear Allie's name. Instead, it had been the opposite.

Luckily, I didn't have too much time to stew over the newspaper articles, since Mama and I had Kelly's funeral to get to. I met Mama right on time at the front office of the motel, said hello to Benny, and soon, we were zipping down the main road that led through Nightmare in Mama's red vintage Mustang.

"Nick and Mia will meet us there," Mama was saying. "Are there any particular people I should chat up for clues?"

Mama made an abrupt right turn, and I reached out to brace myself against the dashboard. Once we were heading in a straight line again, I said, "No. I'm convinced this murder is related to the murder of that other saloon girl last year, but I don't know how."

"Well, Detective Motor Lodge Mama is on the case, so I'll let you know if I hear any tasty bits of gossip. In the meantime, tell me your theories while I drive."

The funeral was being held at a massive stone church about half a mile southwest of High Noon Boulevard. I hadn't ventured to that side of town yet. The church and the houses around it looked historic, but not quite as old as the tourist district. When I commented on that, Mama nodded. "This neighborhood was one of the last to be built before the mine went bust. Some of these houses were never even lived in until the town started making its comeback about forty years ago."

Mama had predicted half of Nightmare would turn out for Kelly's funeral, and it was obvious from the lack of parking that she was right. I doubted it was because Kelly had been popular. Rather, I figured everyone wanted a front-row seat to the scandal and gossip.

We eventually had to park three streets over and hike to the church. We found Nick and Mia waiting for us outside. Both of them were dressed in black, as was Mama. I didn't have anything in my meager wardrobe that was appropriate for a funeral, so I had done my best by donning tailored black trousers—a holdover from my days working in marketing in Nashville—and a gray silk blouse.

The funeral was fairly straightforward, and I found myself getting bored well before the preacher wrapped up. Not only did I not see any suspicious behavior, but I felt like I was in danger of nodding off.

We had been sitting near the back, so when the funeral was over, the four of us were some of the first out the door. We found a shady spot under a nearby eucalyptus tree, and Mama raised an eyebrow at me. "Do you want to do some sleuthing at the cemetery, too?"

"Nah. I don't think there's any need to go to the graveside service."

"How about an early dinner, then? We can get takeout from Spaghetti Western on our way back, then eat in the office with Benny."

I instantly agreed to the idea, since it meant I could enjoy good company and a good meal before I headed to work for the evening. Mia begged off because she had a hair appointment, but Nick agreed to join us as soon as he had picked up Lucy from a friend's house, where she had gone after school.

With our plan set, we began to move toward the sidewalk, but all four of us stopped short when we saw the crowd of people who had gathered there. There was a buzz of angry voices coming from the group, and I distinctly heard one woman say, "Two of my girls have been murdered in just one year!"

"That's Kate. She's a manager at the saloon," Mama whispered to me.

There were some grumbles of agreement, and another voice piped up with, "How can the police not have any viable leads yet? It's ridiculous!"

A few people shouted in agreement. I couldn't blame people for being upset. Of course they wanted answers. The first woman I had heard, Kate, spoke again. "There's a serial killer in Nightmare."

That idea seemed utterly ridiculous to me, until I stopped to think about it. Two saloon girls, both turning up dead at the saloon itself, almost exactly one year apart. Yeah, those circumstances did sound like the work of a serial killer.

Unfortunately, someone else in the crowd had to take it one step further. It was a man with slicked-back hair and sharp little eyes, whose voice rose above everyone else's. "The killer isn't one of us. These murders both happened while that singer just so happened to be in town."

The babble of voices rose, and among the words I caught, one of them stood out to me: *Sanctuary*.

Suddenly, the man with the slicked-back hair turned his eyes on me and pointed. "*She* works there. She can tell us."

It felt like my heart stopped beating entirely, and my

vision narrowed until all I could see was the man's eyes and his hook nose. Vaguely, I felt Mama's hand take mine.

The group began to move as one, like an angry amoeba, in my direction. Soon, there was a wall of people right in front of me. "You're harboring a killer at that creepy haunted house," Kate spat. Her mascara was streaked down her cheeks from crying, and it gave her a villainous look.

I opened my mouth to speak, but absolutely nothing came out.

Mama, on the other hand, had plenty to say. "Kate Barnes, you stop throwing accusations around. You don't know who killed Kelly any more than the rest of us. And if you have any inquiries to make about Nightmare Sanctuary Haunted House, you can direct them to Damien Shackleford. Who, you should remember, is currently running the place because his father is missing. Do you really want to add to his troubles by accusing someone at his business of murder?"

Kate jerked back as if Mama had physically struck her, and she looked down at the ground. "Sorry, Mama," she said in a cowed voice.

"I'm not sorry," shouted another woman. She pushed her way past Kate to glare at Mama. "That singer is guilty! If the police won't do anything about it, then maybe we should."

There were shouts of agreement, and one deep voice piped up with, "Let's go there now to get a confession out of her!"

I was still unable to get a single word out of my mouth. All this group needed was some pitchforks, and they would look like a stereotypical mob. What had I done? What had Justine and I been thinking to bring Allie and Jon to the Sanctuary with us? I had been worried the two of them or the possible vampire slayer might put my co-workers in danger. I hadn't considered I'd be making them a target for the entire town.

"Everybody settle down!" I turned in the direction of the voice and was relieved to see Officer Reyes. He was wearing what must have been the Nightmare Police Department's dress uniform, right down to the cap on his head. "No one is going to threaten anybody else, unless you want to get arrested."

"We're not going to threaten the singer," said the man with the slicked-back hair. "We're just going to ask her some questions."

A few of the people in the group began moving in the direction of the street, as if they were going to jump in their cars and head for the Sanctuary right then and there, even as Officer Reyes and a couple other officers shouted for everyone to remain calm. No one was listening to them.

Everyone fell silent as a woman's voice rose above the din. "Pipe down, all of you!"

As one, the group turned, and I could see the woman who had been hugging Miguel at the vigil in front of the saloon. His mother, I was certain. He was standing right next to her again, wearing a black suit and a black fedora.

The silence stretched as Miguel's mother slowly eyed the ringleaders of the mob with disapproval. When she spoke again, her words were slow and confident. "I don't know who killed Kelly, but that singer had nothing to do with Sarah's death. Kelly killed her."

CHAPTER SIXTEEN

The angry mob turned into a stunned mob in the span of a second. Everyone was staring at Miguel's mother, and I felt Mama's fingers twitch in surprise.

Officer Reyes put his hands on his hips. "Lottie, are you accusing the deceased of murder?"

Lottie nodded her head, her high black bun bobbing rhythmically.

"If you have evidence Kelly Lowry killed Sarah Alton, then why haven't you come to the police with it?"

Lottie squared her shoulders. "I don't have concrete evidence," she said proudly. "I just put the pieces together."

Reyes looked like he was restraining himself from rolling his eyes as he gestured toward Lottie and said, "Please, tell us what you've figured out that the police department didn't."

Lottie looked at the faces around her, her bluster seeming to melt into hesitation. "Kelly and Sarah were best friends. Or they were, until Sarah started dating my son. Kelly was jealous, and she and Sarah had a huge falling out over it."

Has Miguel dated every girl who works at the saloon? I wondered.

Reyes narrowed his eyes at Lottie. "You think Kelly

killed Sarah because she was Miguel's girlfriend. Do you really believe Kelly was jealous enough to kill someone?"

"Oh, she was jealous all right! Kelly once threatened Sarah with a broken beer glass, saying she would slit her throat if she didn't break it off with Miguel."

Miguel had been standing sullenly next to his mother the entire time she was talking, his eyes fixed on the ground and his jaw clenching over and over again. He looked like he was going to explode, so I was surprised how quiet his voice was when he spoke. "Kelly would have never killed anyone. Yes, she threatened Sarah, but she never hurt her, or anyone else. How can you say such horrible things about either one of them?"

Lottie raised a shaking hand and put it on Miguel's shoulder. "I'm sorry you have to learn about it like this. I tried to shield you from the truth, but now that Kelly is dead, there's no reason to hide it anymore."

"Except it's not the truth," I muttered under my breath.

Mama leaned her head close to mine and said in an undertone, "Hush."

Reyes asked Lottie to stop by the police station to give a formal statement, and the crowd began to break up after that. In the wake of Lottie's bombshell, the people seemed to forget they had been planning to storm the Sanctuary. Some people looked shocked and disbelieving, while others were nodding, like it was no surprise.

Once it was just Mama, Nick, Mia, and me standing there, Mama finally released my hand. "I shushed you because I didn't want you to call more attention to yourself. It's lucky for you and for everyone at the haunted house that Lottie distracted those people."

"You're right," I conceded. "But what Lottie said might not be true. It's just speculation, and if you ask me, it seems far-fetched."

"So? It's not your case to solve."

"You're right," I repeated.

"And you need to be careful working under the same roof as that singer. Even if Kelly did kill that other girl, we still don't know who killed Kelly!"

I opened my mouth to tell Mama she was, again, right, but I stopped myself. Instead, I sighed, my mind running over the possibilities this news opened up. Miguel had dated both victims, so he was more suspicious than ever, as far as I was concerned. I found it especially strange that he had referred to Sarah as "the body." Was Miguel afraid that I—or the police—would suspect him if it was widely known he had dated Sarah, too? Why else would he have told me about the murder of his girlfriend in such cold, sterile terms? He hadn't even said her name during our discussion about it.

Maybe the two murders really were the work of a serial killer, and that killer was Miguel.

Maybe his ex-girlfriend Tara would be next.

"I spoke to Miguel again the other day," I said, more to myself than my companions. "He talked about Sarah's death but never once mentioned they had dated."

"Frankly, I hope Kelly really did kill Sarah," Mia said. When I looked at her in surprise, she explained, "It would be one murder solved, and in the meantime, I'll sleep better if I think there's at least one killer who won't be stalking around Nightmare."

Mia left us after that, hurrying to her car to get to the hair salon on time. As she waved goodbye, she laughed and said her client would love hearing about the funeral excitement while having her hair set in rollers.

I, on the other hand, found it hard to be as flippant as Mia. The whole situation was sad and strange. My only consolation was that I mentally checked "vampire slayer" off my list of suspects for good. Mama said something again about having an early dinner, but I declined. I wanted some quiet time to myself.

There were only a couple of hours between the time I got back to my apartment and the time I had to leave for work. Felipe had fallen asleep next to Mori, so I set an alarm and curled up on the love seat for a nap. I dreamed I lived in a castle, and a mob waving torches and pitchforks showed up at my raised drawbridge, demanding I send out the monster so they could "take care of it."

Needless to say, I didn't wake up feeling refreshed. Rather, I felt like I needed a nap to recover from my nap. Even taking Felipe for an afternoon walk didn't do much to perk me up.

During the drive to the Sanctuary, I filled Mori in on everything that had happened at the funeral. I wasn't sure how I had expected her to react, but she laughed heartily when I told her about Lottie's suspicions.

"I love this town so much!" Mori roared. "It reminds me of a village I used to live in, back in France. Every little thing that happened in that village was turned into something far larger than it should have been. I had high hopes for more of the same when I got to Paris, but in the big city, people were too busy to gossip and embellish stories about all their neighbors. It seemed boring by comparison."

"When were you in Paris?" I asked.

"I lived there off and on for many years. The stories I could tell you about the French Revolution!"

"Did you ever mesmerize Napoleon to get a sip of his blood?" I asked, snickering at my own joke.

Mori just gave me a sly glance, her small, wicked smile revealing only the tips of her fangs. She refused to tell me anything, saying it was a story best shared over a drink at Under the Undertaker's.

After we parked, we got out and walked toward the

entrance of the former hospital. It was only as I was reaching out to grab the door handle that I realized the ticket window was still closed. I was surprised since Zach usually had it open pretty early. Still, I brushed it off as no big deal. I popped into the staff restroom to stash my purse in one of the lockers there, then rejoined Mori and Felipe, who had waited for me.

Even before Mori and I reached the open door that led into the dining room, I could hear the buzz of voices coming from inside. It seemed to excite Felipe, who darted ahead of us. Inside, two side-by-side tables were full of Sanctuary residents, and others were standing in a loose circle around them.

Mori strode forward. "What's going on? Is everything okay?"

"For now," Justine said. She always looked in control, even in the most stressful of situations, except at the moment. Her beautiful hair had been twisted up into a messy bun and secured with a pencil. As I watched, she pulled the pencil out and began to chew on the eraser nervously as her hair spilled down her back in tangles.

"It's my fault," Allie said. She was standing just in front of me, and when she turned around, I could see the way her lip quivered. "Some people in this town believe I killed Kelly, and they thought a little vigilante justice was in order."

"Oh," I said flatly. "The gossip about the funeral has made it out here, I see."

"You already heard about it?" Justine asked.

"I was there."

Malcolm rose from one of the benches. "Were you harmed?"

I waved my hands. "No. No one got hurt at the funeral. I was in grave danger of being yelled at a lot, but Mama—Sue Dalton over at Cowboy's Corral—gave the people doing the yelling a good telling-off. It was scary, though."

"She did the right thing." Damien was sitting at one end of the table farthest from me, and I had to lean slightly to get a glimpse of him through the crowd. "Mama called me a bit ago, and she said she told those folks that if someone had an issue with the Sanctuary or anyone in it, they could contact me. And they have. I was going to save this for the meeting, but there's no point in waiting. I've gotten death threats all afternoon. Some directed toward me, some toward Allie. Everyone needs to be alert tonight. I think those people were all talk, but better safe than sorry."

"I can't believe you're still going to open your doors tonight," Jon said angrily. "How do you plan to keep Allie safe?"

"She's going to stay in my office, with me, from the time the first tourist walks through that door until the last one leaves." Damien's voice was firm, and I had learned to detect the edge of anger in his tone when he felt like someone was trying to overstep his authority.

"That's not good enough," Jon spat.

Mori and I exchanged wide-eyed looks. Did Jon not realize the folly of going up against Damien?

"Fine," Damien said coolly. "You can join us. I had thought you wanted to work in the haunt to make some money, but I respect that Allie's safety is more important to you. Bring a book. It will be a long evening."

Jon looked like he was going to retort, but Justine reached toward him and shook her head slightly in warning.

Damien turned and began to stalk out of the dining room. As he went, he growled, "Olivia, come with me."

Uh-oh. I'm in trouble.

I followed Damien at a slower pace, hoping to put off

whatever lecture he was about to give me for as long as possible. He was already seated at his desk by the time I got to his office, and I automatically closed the door behind me. Even if Damien didn't want privacy, I did.

"You'll be practicing with me this evening," he said without preamble.

Whatever I had been expecting him to say, it wasn't that. "What?"

"I know you're busy trying to clear Allie's name, but you still need to work on controlling your conjuring skills. I think you should do both. You'll be in here, with me, tonight."

I frowned. "You want me to try my alleged abilities on Allie?"

Damien nodded. "We're not going to tell her or that fussy manager, but I want your focus tonight to be on getting the truth from Allie. From eight o'clock until midnight, I want your greatest wish in the world to be learning whether she killed someone."

I nodded. It would be fruitless to point out—for the five millionth time—that I didn't have any abilities. Still, if I could be in close proximity to Allie and Jon for four hours, maybe one of them would let something slip, some little comment that might be useful. "Deal," I told Damien. "I'm going to the family meeting first, in case I need to know anything relevant. I'll also let Justine know someone will have to fill in for me tonight."

After the meeting, I stepped into the restroom to retrieve my purse from my locker. There was a bench in front of the row of lockers, and I was surprised to see a note with my name on it sitting there. I picked up the sheet of paper, which was folded in half, and opened it warily.

If you care at all about Allie, stop looking for Sarah Alton's killer.

CHAPTER SEVENTEEN

I clutched the note to my chest and looked around wildly to see if anyone was in there with me. I appeared to be alone, so I stuffed the note into my purse and headed back to Damien's office. I tried to walk quickly, but not so quickly I called attention to myself.

Thankfully, Damien was still alone in his office. The Sanctuary wouldn't open to guests for another ten minutes, and I hoped Allie and Jon would wait until the last possible second to show up.

I slammed Damien's door behind me as I hurried to his desk. "Look," I said breathlessly as I pulled the note out of my purse and flattened it on the desk. "I just found this in front of the lockers. I'm guessing I wasn't supposed to find it until tonight, after work."

"This makes Allie look guilty of that first murder." Damien was stating the obvious.

"And Jon had to be the one who wrote the note. Who else would be so worried about Allie? But he must have known I would immediately think of him, so why bother leaving me an unsigned note by my locker? It's even written like he wanted to disguise his handwriting."

"I can't imagine who else here would write something like that, unless…"

"Unless what?" I asked impatiently.

Damien was silent for a long time, but when I continued to stare him down, he said reluctantly, "I was thinking maybe someone who works here was responsible for that first murder, and they don't want their guilt to be uncovered, so they're trying to make you stop poking into it."

I didn't even dignify that with an answer. I just pursed my lips and gave Damien my best judgmental glare.

"I knew you'd react like that if I said it," he grumbled.

The adrenaline was starting to wear off, and I sank down into one of the chairs. "You were right." *How many times am I going to say that today?* "Justine and I only made more trouble by telling Allie and Jon to stay here."

Damien smiled faintly. "When all of this is over, and everyone here is safe, I'm going to say, 'I told you so.'"

"I won't even argue with you when you do."

Damien half rose so he could push the button he'd used before to call Tanner and McCrory. "Let's see what our spies have observed," he said.

The two ghosts materialized about a minute later. McCrory gave us a polite nod, but Tanner complained, "You're interrupting an epic poker game."

"Funny, I would think you're too busy watching our guests to play poker," Damien retorted.

Tanner shrugged. "They went to the nightly meeting in the dining room, so we took a break. No point spying on them in there, where you living folks can do it."

I sighed and looked at Damien. "That means they didn't see who left that note for me."

"Have you noticed anything unusual when you're actually doing the work you're supposed to be doing?" Damien asked.

McCrory straightened up and bowed his chest out. "Listen here, Mr. Shackleford. We've been real good about tracking those two, but so far, we haven't seen or heard anything to make us think they're up to something."

"Yeah," Tanner said, "the only weird thing is the way that vamp drinks blood. Right out of a cup, like she's having a whiskey." The red bandana over his face twitched, and I imagined he was making a face of disgust under there.

I looked at Damien. "If we don't learn anything helpful tonight, I think we need to try other people from Kelly's life. After the bombshell Miguel's mother dropped today, I'd love to have a chat with her."

"If you do, then I'm going with you."

Before I could protest, there was a firm knock on the door. Damien looked at Tanner and McCrory and said quietly, "You're free until midnight. Get back to your poker game, now." The two ghosts didn't argue. They sailed through the wall without another word.

Allie and Jon both looked surprised to see me sitting in Damien's office. While Allie appeared only mildly interested, though, Jon's expression turned sour. Well, more sour than it already was. He seemed to be carrying a grudge, though when everyone at the Sanctuary was being so kind to him and Allie, I couldn't understand why.

As a matter of fact, he reminded me a bit of Damien. It was amazing the two of them weren't best friends already.

Damien told Allie and Jon I was there to practice my conjuring skills to help us find Baxter, and Allie's face lit up. "Ooh, I've heard of conjurors, but I've never met one! How exciting!"

I shook my head. "No, I don't really have any skills. Damien is exaggerating, a lot."

"If I had your abilities, I would be living in a mansion in the mountains. Oh, and I would have a huge outdoor stage so I could host nighttime concerts there! What have you conjured into your life?"

I laughed so hard I actually had to reach up and wipe a tear from my eye. When I calmed down, I said, "A divorce, a house foreclosure, and a cleaned-out retirement account." I shook my head. "I haven't conjured anything. Like I just said, I don't have any conjuring skills."

"Don't listen to her," Damien growled, obviously annoyed with me. "Olivia conjured her job here, and she conjured herself a free apartment."

My brow furrowed, but I kept my mouth shut. My apartment wasn't free. I was trading marketing work for it. Implying I had just made a wish and it happened by magic made me feel small, like my actual skills weren't of any real value.

However, I knew this was not the time to get into another argument with Damien. Instead, I acted like the dutiful little conjuring student. He handed me an old leather-bound journal that had a long red ribbon tied around it. "It's my father's," Damien said solemnly. "I haven't read it, but I believe this was one of his journals. While you read it, focus on him and how much you want to find him."

My hands shook slightly as I untied the ribbon and set it on the edge of the desk. I glanced at Allie and Jon, but they didn't seem to be paying attention. Allie had brought her guitar and a book with her, and she was sitting in the chair next to me, already reading. Jon was pacing back and forth behind us.

I had two choices: I could focus my intent on finding Baxter, or I could concentrate on getting definitive answers out of Allie about the murder. I suspected the journal was just a cover Damien was using so it would look like I was practicing my skills on finding his father, when in fact I would be exercising my ability to get Allie to talk about murder.

Except I don't have any abilities. Sometimes, Damien's absolute faith in my skills made me start to believe, too, and I had to remind myself that wasn't the case. I realized I had three choices rather than just two, with the third being not concentrating on anything at all. I was curious to read Baxter's journal, and I could happily occupy myself with that for the next couple of hours.

Is it possible to give off rebellious vibes? If so, I must have been doing it, because Damien cleared his throat. I looked up to see him glaring at me, and there was a faint green glow to his eyes.

He was angry. I had only seen Damien's eyes glow when he was angry or upset, and for some reason, he was angry at me. I pointed discreetly at my own eyes and mouthed, "Glowing." Damien's shoulders jerked in surprise. I expected him to put on his mirrored sunglasses, but instead, he rose and went to one of the bookcases. As he stood there like he was perusing the titles, I could see the way he was taking deep breaths and knew he was trying to calm himself down.

I just couldn't figure out how he had known I was reluctant to practice my so-called skills, and I certainly didn't know why it had upset him so much. With a sigh, I opened the front cover of the journal, its black leather soft under my fingers, and turned my attention to the first page. I told myself I would read a little bit, then focus my attention on Allie and my wish for her to give me helpful information about Kelly's murder.

After all, I had told Damien I would.

The writing in the journal was familiar to me since it was the same I had seen on the job listing at the Nightmare Chamber of Commerce. Damien had told me it was Baxter's thin, slanted writing on that notecard, and this journal entry was definitely a match. The entry was dated June 14, 1962.

We buried the siren today in the old Nightmare Sanctuary Hospital and Asylum cemetery.

When I gasped, Damien instantly turned to me. "What?"

"There was a siren here before Seraphina!"

Damien's expression relaxed. "Oh, yeah. Some of the old-timers talk about her. She lived to be nearly a hundred. Apparently, by the time she died, the scales on her tail were losing their color."

Talking casually about an old-lady siren felt surreal, and I just muttered a quiet "*huh*" before turning my attention back to the page. Before I could read more, though, Damien knelt down next to me. I instinctively leaned toward him.

Damien's eyes flashed again, ever so slightly. "If there's anything in there about my mother, don't tell me," he whispered.

Oh. Oh, wow. I had totally misread Damien's emotions as anger toward me, when in fact he was afraid. He'd already been sucker punched by the living quarters in the mine and the photo of his mom, and he didn't want to take another hit.

I stopped reading after that, worried I would, in fact, learn something about Damien's mom, and I wouldn't be able to keep it a secret. I had never had a good poker face. Instead, I stared down at the rug, turning a page of the journal every few minutes so it looked like I was reading, and thought over and over again how much I wanted Allie to start talking. I even visualized her letting something slip while we were sitting there next to each other.

Unfortunately, she barely uttered a peep for the next two hours. She was reading when Damien sent me out to relieve some of the people working inside the haunt so they could take their breaks. I took turns at the front door and the exit, and I lurked in the shadows of the cemetery scene while Fiona was on break. I donned a billowy gray dress with a hood for that one, which slipped right on over my jeans and Nightmare Sanctuary T-shirt. I tried my best to scare the guests who came through, but there was no competing with a real banshee.

When I got back from my rounds, Allie was still reading. The only change was that Jon had finally settled down. He was sitting in my chair with headphones on. I didn't bother to shoo him out of the spot. I was getting frustrated, so I took up the pacing for a while.

The night absolutely dragged by, and when we got word the last tourist had exited the building shortly after midnight, I sighed in defeat. Allie and Jon said a quick good night and disappeared, and I turned to Damien. "I tried. I really did."

"I believe you." Damien picked up the journal from the corner of his desk, where I had left it. "Did you find anything interesting?"

I confessed I had stopped reading after that first line, and Damien seemed almost relieved. He retied the ribbon around the journal and slid it into a desk drawer.

There was nothing to discuss with Damien since we had gotten absolutely nowhere during the night, so I was soon walking through the entryway toward the front doors, where I had made plans to meet Mori and Felipe. Madge, Maida, and Morgan were all coming from the direction of the entrance to the haunt, and our paths crossed right in the middle of the room.

"Olivia, a moment, please," Madge said.

When I stopped, Maida looked up at me ominously. "Knowledge is dangerous in the wrong hands."

"Power with ill intent is deadly," Morgan added, her wrinkled hands curling into fists.

I looked at Madge, hoping she would interpret for the other two witches' cryptic words. "I had an unexpected visitor this afternoon," she said. "Allie's manager came to me, wanting to know if I could teach him how to hypnotize someone."

CHAPTER EIGHTEEN

"Why in the world would Jon be asking about hypnotism?" I asked. Mentally, I was already coming up with a list of possibilities, and none of them were good.

"He didn't say," Madge said. "I told him that's not something a moral witch would share with just anyone."

"It's something you know how to do, though?" I remembered Madge had once threatened someone with a truth-telling spell, and I suddenly felt excited. "Can you use your truth-telling spell on Jon and Allie? Maybe we can find out if they know more about the murder than they're letting on!"

Madge was already shaking her head firmly before I had even finished talking. "Oh, no. It's really not an ethical thing to do. When I said I would use it on Robert, er, I mean, Cowan, it was because I was so upset. My ex-boyfriend had shown up here armed and ready to do battle with Nightmare's supernatural community. I was a bit on edge that night."

I was disappointed with that answer, but I could appreciate Madge's refusal and the fact there were ethics to being a witch. It was something she obviously took seriously.

"But we'll keep watch," Maida said. "Kids make great spies, because no one thinks we're listening to them." She grinned at me, and I felt a shiver work its way up my spine. She was sweet, but she was also a little scary.

"And people tend to let things slip around old ladies," Morgan said. "It's quite the advantage for me."

I thanked the witches for their vigilance, and they left, heading upstairs to their apartment. Between the strange note in the locker room and Jon wanting to know about hypnotism, he was looking mighty suspicious. I didn't want to think he was a murderer, but at the moment, he seemed more likely than even Miguel, the serial saloon-girl dater.

Mori and Felipe joined me soon after, and on the drive back to Cowboy's Corral, I filled Mori in on the events of the evening. In response, she just said, "I made the right decision to stay at your place."

That night, I didn't have any more strange dreams. Or if I did, I was sleeping so deeply I didn't remember them. I barely even remembered getting up at dawn to move to the love seat.

I didn't wake up completely until my cell phone started ringing. By that point, I was curled up in a ball on the love seat with a blanket tucked in around me and Felipe perched on top of my legs. I heard him snoring softly as I groped for the phone with one hand.

It was Damien. "Do you still want to talk to the mother of the boyfriend?" he asked.

"Lottie. And yeah, I do." I started gently pushing against Felipe, trying to wake him so I could sit up.

"She's been at the saloon since it opened this morning, at least according to the bank teller I just talked to. This might be a great chance to have a chat with her, because it sounds like she's over there getting pretty loosened up."

"That means we should go talk to her before she's too drunk to make any sense." Felipe was finally awake, and I slid him off me. "I'll get ready and head over there."

"I said I would go with you to talk to her, remember?"

"Okay, then meet me there in about thirty minutes."

"I'm already parked outside your apartment. Be down in ten."

I really wanted to take a shower, but I settled for washing my face and running a brush through my hair. When I did emerge, I had Felipe on a leash. Damien was leaning against his Corvette, and he cocked his head when he saw us coming down the stairs.

"He needs a quick walk," I explained. It was already nearly eleven o'clock in the morning, which meant there were a lot more people around than the past couple of times I had walked Felipe. I hustled him to the back alley, and luckily, we didn't cross paths with anyone.

Once Felipe was back in the apartment and settled in on the love seat again, I rejoined Damien. "You're awfully excited about this," I said, yawning. "You didn't even give me enough time to have coffee."

"I'm not excited. I'm just ready to have this entire ordeal over with. Let's go."

The saloon was close enough that the drive took only a few minutes, and half of that time was finding parking. It was Friday, which meant weekend tourists were beginning to arrive. The saloon was already crowded with them, all eager to drink beer in the same place where outlaws like Butch Tanner once had.

Lottie was at a table in a corner of the saloon, half hidden by the upright piano against the wall. She was sitting by herself, and there were three empty glasses in front of her. She was about halfway through a fourth.

"Hello again, Lottie," I said brightly as I slid into one of the empty chairs at the table. "May I join you?"

"You already did," Lottie answered flatly.

"Damien is going to get us some drinks. Would you like anything?"

In answer, Lottie waved her glass in the air and pointed at it with her free hand.

Damien nodded curtly. "Three sarsaparillas it is."

While Damien headed toward the bar, I leaned in toward Lottie and asked, "You okay?"

"What's it to you?"

"It's not even noon yet, and you're on your fourth beer. Your son's girlfriend was murdered earlier this week, and you think she was a killer herself. I'm just asking if you're doing okay."

"I already told the police everything, so why would I answer to you? You're that lady who sticks her nose into other people's business." Lottie took a big swig, hiccupped, and added, "Besides, you're housing that singer at your place for weird people. I don't trust you."

Seeing an opportunity, I leaned toward Lottie and said conspiratorially, "And I don't trust 'that singer,' as you say. I think she might have had something to do with Kelly's death, which is why I wanted to talk to you."

Lottie's eyes focused on me for a brief moment. "Neither one of them was good enough for my boy. Sarah and Kelly were both trouble. I had warned him to stay away from the girls who work here, but he wouldn't listen."

I nodded my head and made one of those sounds that only middle-aged women can make about the younger generation's decisions. "He dated both Sarah and Kelly, but I understand he dated Tara for a few months, too."

That seemed to rile Lottie up, and she slammed her glass down on the table hard enough that some of the beer sloshed out. "She was definitely never good enough for Miguel. But what could I say? Sarah had just been murdered, and Miguel was heartbroken about losing her. It's no surprise he fell into the arms of the nearest woman. We all knew it wouldn't last long."

I held up one finger. "Miguel's girlfriend Sarah was

murdered a year ago." I held up a second finger. "Then he dated Tara for a few months."

Even as I was raising a third finger, Lottie was already beginning to talk. "I know. Three girlfriends in only one year, and two of them murdered. I realize it doesn't look good for my son, but believe me, he had nothing to do with their deaths. He's a good boy."

Sure. A good boy in a biker gang who has two dead girlfriends.

Damien returned with our drinks just then, and Lottie frowned at the glass he put down in front of her. She leaned forward and sniffed at the liquid inside, then grimaced. "This isn't beer."

"I told you I was getting a round of sarsaparillas."

Lottie pushed the glass away angrily, then drained the rest of her beer. "Leave me alone. I'll find someone who can bring me a real drink."

"Before we go, though," I said hastily, "I just have one more question. Do you really believe Kelly killed Sarah?"

"Of course I do. Now go away."

I realized continuing to question Lottie would be futile, so Damien and I grabbed our drinks and headed for the bar, where we found two open barstools. I sipped at my drink moodily. I had hoped to get more out of Lottie, especially regarding her belief Kelly was a killer before she was ever a victim. Damien seemed to sense I was in a bad mood, because he remained silent.

I was just draining my glass when there was a tap on my shoulder. I spun around on my barstool to see Miguel standing there, looking abashed. "I came to collect my mom," he said, glancing in her direction.

"She must be more broken up about Kelly's death than she's letting on," I said.

"I think she's upset because the police are asking me a lot of tough questions." Miguel hesitated, then said, "In fact, that's the reason I was planning to track you down later today, but here you are."

"Track me down? Why?"

"You've helped with other murders. And, honestly, I don't want your help to prove my innocence, but Kelly's. I just can't believe she would ever kill anyone, especially Sarah. They were once such close friends."

I laughed quietly. "If you're trying to hire me as your own PI, you've come to the wrong person. I'm anxious to get this whole thing over with, too, but I haven't been finding much useful information."

"All I'm asking is that you help me get some time with Allie. Kelly was working her dressing room the night Sarah was killed, and I'm hoping Allie might remember something helpful or be able to provide an alibi for Kelly. I just want to find out what Allie knows."

"You and me, both," I mumbled.

"Sarah's body was moved after her killer thought she was dead, according to the police," Miguel continued doggedly. "I seriously doubt Kelly would have been strong enough to carry a mostly dead person to that spot behind the dumpster."

Damien had been listening to the exchange silently, still facing the bar. At that mention, he turned around slowly on his stool. "Did somebody move the body to the alley in order to frame someone at the saloon?"

Miguel narrowed his eyes at Damien, and I quickly said, "This is Damien Shackleford. His dad owns the Sanctuary. He's as eager to find the truth as you and me."

Miguel looked Damien up and down, taking in his black suit, which was way too fancy for the saloon. Eventually, he nodded once, then leaned in toward both of us. "The police think she was killed somewhere else, then her body was stashed behind the dumpster in the alley. So, yes, it's possible her killer was trying to frame someone at the saloon, or perhaps Allie herself, though the police say—" Miguel broke off, cleared his throat, and continued, "Sarah wasn't dead yet, so she crawled to the saloon door, hoping someone would come to her rescue."

That horrific detail wasn't new to me since I had read it in the newspaper, but it didn't make sense to me that Sarah had been killed anywhere but right there behind the dumpster. "Why do the police think Sarah was killed elsewhere?" I asked.

"Because there was no blood where they found her. Not on Sarah, not on the ground around her, and not anywhere around the dumpster."

CHAPTER NINETEEN

I turned toward Damien, and his eyes met mine for the briefest second. I knew he was thinking the same thing I was: there was no blood on or near Sarah because she had been drained by a vampire. Was this why Jon had mentioned Allie couldn't feed properly as long as they were in Nightmare? Maybe he knew she had killed Sarah. Maybe she wasn't good at stopping before she killed the people she was feeding from, and Jon was worried that yet another dead body might turn up in Nightmare.

If Allie really was that sloppy, then it was no wonder Jon followed her around in a constant nervous tizzy.

None of those details explained who had killed Kelly, or why, but I felt like we were finally getting somewhere regarding Sarah's murder. Unfortunately, that somewhere wasn't where I wanted to go.

There was no way I could share my suspicion with Miguel, so I said, in as casual of a tone as I could muster, "I didn't read about this alleged pre-dumpster site when I looked at newspaper articles from last year."

"The police didn't broadcast those details. I think they were embarrassed that they had a body but no crime scene. I saw Sarah that night, just before she went to work. She was with me at the coffee shop, and then she went right down the street to the saloon. She was already in this area, so it makes no sense that she would have been killed a long distance from here. The original crime scene should have been close by, and it should have been easy to find."

"Perhaps she was killed indoors, but everything was cleaned up too well for the police to identify the right spot," Damien suggested.

Miguel laughed darkly. "Right, all that blood she lost just disappeared."

Again, Damien and I exchanged a glance. There had probably been no blood to clean up. I was thinking it, and I knew he was, too.

We were interrupted by the sound of someone banging on the piano keys, the clashing chord silencing everyone at the saloon. Every single head turned to stare at Lottie, who slammed her fingers down onto the keys again and lifted her head. "Ohhh," she sang loudly.

Miguel ran over to her as fast as he could, and after what appeared to be some protesting on Lottie's part, he led her out of the saloon, one arm clamped tightly around her shoulders.

Damien drove me back to the motel after that. We agreed it was looking like Allie was guilty of at least one murder. "I'm going to be waiting for her tonight. The second the sun goes down, she's going to wake up, and I'll be the first thing she sees," Damien said firmly.

"I'll be right there with you. I'll walk over early. Mori can drive over in my car later."

I spent most of my afternoon in the front office of the motel. Mama had, somehow, already heard the gossip about Lottie's "performance" at the saloon, and I told her Damien and I had witnessed the whole thing. Just as soon as I finished giving her the details about it, Mama leaned over the countertop with a sly look. "So you and Damien were hanging out at the saloon, huh?"

I raised my hands, palms out to ward off her implication. "No. We weren't hanging out. We went to talk to Lottie, because Damien had heard she was there."

Mama rolled her eyes. "You're still trying to solve this murder."

"I'm still trying to make sure the two people currently staying at the place I work aren't guilty of it."

"Fair enough." Mama paused, then said, "I appreciate that you're giving him a chance."

Ugh. I just didn't get why Mama was such a cheerleader for Damien. "I'm trying," I told her. I meant it, too.

When it was time for me to head to the Sanctuary, I wrote a note for Mori, explaining I was leaving early and that my car keys were on the kitchen table for her. I walked Felipe, then began my own walk to work.

I had made the trip, either on foot or in my car, so many times by this point that I rarely paid attention to the gallows at the crossroads, where I turned right onto the dirt lane that led to the Sanctuary. On this day, though, they seemed to stand out from their surroundings. Maybe it was because the sun was still above the mountains on the horizon, so they were backlit dramatically, or maybe my mood brought them to my attention. Either way, the scene looked ominous.

When I walked inside the Sanctuary, it was eerily quiet. I wasn't used to getting to work so early. The vampires were asleep at that hour, though Mori and Theo were doing their sleeping elsewhere. As for the others, most of them were just beginning their day, so they were probably upstairs in their rooms or apartments, getting ready for the evening's work.

I popped my head into the ticket office since the window outside had been closed. Zach was seated there, with a big stack of receipts in front of him. "Hey," I called. "Have things been quiet today?"

Zach didn't look up at me as he said, "Yup."

I was turning to leave when Zach called my name. I looked over my shoulder at him, one eyebrow raised.

"I went to The Lusty for lunch today," he began. "I sometimes get cravings for rare meat, and the lunchtime cook there knows just how to make a cheeseburger for me."

"Yuck."

Zach waved a hand dismissively. "It's a werewolf thing. Anyway, your friend Ella was my server at the counter. She said she knows you're interested in this murder, and she asked me to pass along a piece of news."

I smiled. "Ella hears a lot of good stuff over there."

"She told me that this morning, one of her breakfast customers was that self-serving real estate agent—"

"Emmett," I supplied. I kind of liked the guy, but Zach's description wasn't wrong.

"And he was with the mother of the dead girl's boyfriend. Lottie, I think Ella called her."

I nodded and made a *keep going* motion with my hand.

"Lottie was going on and on about how she had no choice but to downsize. Ella heard enough to know Emmett is helping her find a smaller, cheaper place to live."

That probably explained why Lottie had been getting drunk at the saloon before lunchtime. She was upset about her finances, not about Kelly's death. Lottie had probably headed straight from The Lusty to the saloon. Still, her conversation with Emmett didn't seem to have anything to do with the murder, and I said so to Zach.

"I'm not finished yet. Emmett asked Lottie if it would just be her living in the new place, and Lottie said yes. She added that even though her son's girlfriend was dead, she expected Miguel would be moving on to the next one pretty quickly."

Zach looked at me expectantly, like he was waiting for a reaction. "That's it," he said.

I still wasn't sure what the story had to do with the murder. Unless, of course, Ella thought the conversation implied Miguel's guilt because Lottie expected him to dive right into another relationship. "Sarah might have been the love of his life," I speculated. "Miguel might have believed Kelly killed her, and he got his revenge. He claims Kelly was innocent, and he seems broken up about her death, but he could be acting like that to make himself look less suspicious."

Zach gestured toward the laptop on his desk. "Hang on, let me start a spreadsheet so I can keep track of all the intrigue," he said sarcastically.

"Sorry. I'm just thinking out loud. Thanks for passing this along, Zach. It could be helpful."

"Oh, you know, being the Sanctuary's accountant, ticket sales manager, and security guard wasn't enough. I wanted to add 'informant' to the list."

I left Zach to whichever job he was currently working and continued down the hall to Damien's office. According to my watch, sunset was in nine minutes.

Damien was sitting at his desk, going over his own stack of receipts. He didn't seem to notice me standing in his doorway, so I said softly, "It's almost time."

"So it is," Damien said, consulting his own watch. "Let's go get a front row seat to Allie's coffin."

As I followed Damien toward the stairs that led down into the basement, I asked him if he was joking about the coffin. "No," he said, sounding surprised I would even ask. "It's the safest place for a vampire to hide from the sun. Mori and Theo have beds in their basement-level apartments, but I understand it took both of them years to come around to the idea of sleeping in anything but a coffin. I'd be willing to bet Allie has one shoved into the back of her tour van."

I thought for a moment. "Oh. Justine and I sat on a huge music case when we rode over here with them. You know, like you see on stage at big concerts. I bet she sleeps in it."

"It would serve the same purpose as a coffin: a secure, dark place. And, if anyone ever peeked inside their van, a music case would blend right in with the rest of the stuff more than a coffin ever could."

"Does the Sanctuary keep extra coffins on hand for guests?" I asked.

Damien nodded. "Of course. There are also cells in the basement with chains, for any visiting creatures who can't control their darker sides."

I shuddered. That seemed slightly barbaric and very frightening. I knew there were supernatural creatures in the world who were dangerous, but I didn't like the idea of any of them visiting Nightmare Sanctuary.

At the bottom of the stairs, there was a hallway leading straight, as well as hallways to the left and right. The right-hand hallway had a big door with a lock, and a sign on it indicated it was storage for props used in the haunt. Straight ahead, the tunnel was dark and dirty, and it gave me the creeps.

Thankfully, Damien turned left, choosing the hallway that looked downright cozy. It had a lush floral carpet, pale green paint on the walls, and framed photographs that I assumed were of various people who had lived and worked at the Sanctuary over the years.

"There's Mori's place," Damien said, pointing at a door on the right. There was a fall-themed wreath hanging on the door. A short distance farther down the hall, Damien gestured to another door. "Theo lives there." A small black pirate flag, complete with a skull and crossbones, was hanging on the wall next to the door. Of course.

"And here we are," Damien said, stopping near the end of the hallway. "The guest quarters."

"Is Jon staying in there, too?" I asked.

"Yeah. We have nice rooms upstairs, but he insisted on dragging a mattress down here so he could keep an eye on Allie. I'm sure he won't be happy to see us."

Damien knocked loudly, and a moment later, Jon's voice called, "Who's there?"

"It's Damien. Open up."

"Just a minute. Just a minute."

Through the door, I could hear muffled shuffling sounds and a few *thunks*. A moment later, Jon answered the door wearing plaid pajama pants and a gray T-shirt. He was dressed for sleep, but he looked wide awake as he deftly slipped into the hallway and shut the door behind him.

"Well?" Jon asked. He pushed his glasses higher up on the bridge of his nose, his lips pursed.

"We're here to have a chat with Allie," Damien said.

"She's not awake yet. Sorry."

Damien smiled in a way that managed to be intimidating. "We'll wait."

Jon had looked like a man on the verge of a nervous breakdown since the day I had met him. In a heartbeat, though, his face twisted in anger. Jon bent his knees and pulled one arm back, turning so his elbow wouldn't hit the door.

Beside me, I felt Damien tense, right before Jon's fist flew toward his face.

CHAPTER TWENTY

I tried to yell, "Look out!" What came out of my mouth instead was more of a yelp, but I shouldn't have worried. One of Damien's hands shot up to intercept the punch, and soon, Damien had Jon pinned against the wall, his arm twisted behind his back.

"Let me go, right now!" Jon shouted, craning his head around to glare at Damien. I instinctively stepped backward when I saw the rage on Jon's face. What had happened to the nervous demeanor?

"Olivia, go get Gunnar and Zach," Damien growled. "Now."

I turned and fled toward the stairs that led out of the basement. By the time I reached the ticket office, I was out of breath and trying not to panic. I wasn't even sure what I was on the verge of panicking about. Damien certainly wasn't in any danger.

Maybe Jon was, though. I didn't particularly care for him, but I also didn't want Damien to hurt him. It wasn't that I thought Damien would intentionally do something to Jon. Rather, I was worried Damien's anger would make his supernatural ability flare up, and he might not be able to control himself.

And this is exactly why Damien is so insistent that I learn to control my emotions.

I pushed that thought out of my head as I shot through the door of the ticket office. Zach looked up at me in surprise.

"Basement! Help! Damien!" I was so out of breath it was all I could get out.

Thankfully, Zach didn't need more than that. He leaped out of his chair and pushed past me, disappearing in the direction of the basement stairs. I wasn't sure where Gunnar would be, so I took a few deep breaths, then headed for the dining room. It was empty.

I went upstairs before realizing I had no idea which apartment was Gunnar's, so I hurried as fast as I could down the hallway along the east wing of the building. I knew where the witches lived since I had been there before, and I knocked on their door when I reached it.

Maida answered the door before I had lowered my hand. "There's trouble," she said in a matter-of-fact tone.

"In the basement. I need Gunnar," I said.

Maida pointed down the hallway. "Second door on your left."

I called a breathless "thanks" as I sprinted to the door Maida had indicated. I banged on the wooden door and called Gunnar's name. "We need you in the basement!" I yelled.

The door opened a second later, and I jumped back as Gunnar barreled into the hallway. Like Zach, Gunnar didn't waste time asking questions. As he raced toward the stairs, I shouted at his back, "Allie's quarters. It's Jon!"

I hurried after Gunnar, hearing the squeak of doors opening in my wake. I knew everyone would be buzzing about this at the family meeting, but at the moment, I didn't care.

By the time I was back where I had started, standing in the basement hallway outside the vampire guest room,

Zach and Gunnar each had one of Jon's arms in their grip. Jon still looked angry, but he wasn't fighting them.

I stopped a short distance away, not keen to be any closer to Jon than I needed to be. As I struggled to catch my breath, the guest room door opened, and Allie appeared. She looked slightly groggy, which made sense since she had just woken up, but she also looked more haggard. Her cheeks seemed a bit hollow, and her skin had a sort of translucence to it.

As soon as Allie saw that Jon was being restrained by Zach and Gunnar, she shook herself and went from looking sleepy to wide awake. "What's going on?" she asked, her head swiveling between Jon and Damien.

"You can't trust him!" Jon shouted. "Don't let him trick you into thinking you're safe here!"

Unlike Jon, Damien spoke calmly. I was relieved his anger had died down, even though I could hear it bubbling just beneath the surface. "Allie, Olivia and I came down here to ask you some questions. We're as anxious to have this murder solved as you are. That's all."

"You're here to accuse her of murder!" Jon's face was beet red, and he twisted his torso in an effort to free himself.

"You do realize," I said, opening my big mouth before I could stop myself, "your reaction to this only makes Allie seem guilty. The harder you try to shield her, the more suspicious she looks." Jon's bizarre behavior, coupled with the note he had left me in the locker room, made me almost certain Allie was, in fact, involved in at least one of the murders.

Everyone's attention was on me, and I suddenly felt self-conscious. Allie was peering at me with an expression that looked worried and uncertain. After a long, silent, awkward moment, she said, "You're right, of course. Jon is making it look like I have something to hide. I assure you, though, I haven't killed anyone."

"You don't need to defend yourself to these people!" Jon had stopped shouting, but his words were shrill and biting.

Allie rounded on Jon, her eyes narrowed. "*These people* have given us a safe place to stay. They're feeding you and letting us work to make a bit of cash. How can you not trust them?"

"I went into town today," Jon said, and I could hear the fear creeping into his voice. *Good,* I thought, *he's getting back to normal.* "Do you know what people are saying about you? There were some men at the coffee shop who were talking about getting a group together to come over here tonight. Damien is only going to put up with us for so long. We're bad for his business."

"No," Damien said. "You're bad for the Sanctuary's relationship with the non-supernatural people in this town. That's dangerous for all of us, but I'm not going to turn you over to a mob or anything ridiculous like that. Like I said, Olivia and I just wanted to have a chat with Allie."

Jon stiffened. "Fine," he spat. "But I'm going to stay with her. She doesn't answer any questions I don't agree with."

"Oh, for—" Allie began. The rest of her words were muffled, but I could hear the frustration. She gazed at Jon, then sighed. "I think you need to walk it off."

"What?" Jon asked incredulously.

"Go outside and calm down. I don't need you to babysit me."

Damien looked at Zach and jerked his head in the direction of the stairs. "Go with him, both of you."

Jon protested as Zach and Gunnar herded him down the hall, but at least they dropped his arms. When the echoes of Jon's protests faded, Allie said quietly, "Let me get dressed, at least. Can I meet you in your office in ten minutes?"

Damien looked like he wanted to argue, but he finally nodded. "Fine. Ten minutes, and not a second more."

As soon as Allie had retreated into her room, Damien called softly, "Tanner. McCrory."

The ghosts materialized a few feet away. "Yeah, boss?" Tanner asked.

"She has ten minutes to get to my office. You let me know if she strays from that plan."

McCrory took off his hat and picked at a spot on the brim. "I sure hope the lady isn't a killer. She seems nice."

"I hope so, too," Damien said.

I followed Damien back to his office, still trying to process what had just happened. We had known Jon wouldn't like us questioning Allie, but certainly, neither one of us had expected such a violent response. I felt sad as I sank down into a chair. I liked Allie. She seemed nice, and I didn't want her to be the villain in this story.

We only had to wait six minutes before Allie arrived. I stood up to see she had changed into a blue gauzy dress that swirled around her knees, and I wondered if she had chosen it because it gave her an aura of sweetness. She didn't look like someone who could kill. I was sure Allie was normally radiant in that dress, but at the moment, its bright color only highlighted her sunken cheeks and beleaguered look.

Allie shut the door and turned to us grimly. "I'm so, so sorry Jon went after you, Damien. After everything you've done for us... that you're still doing for us..." She trailed off and shook her head sadly.

"It's not your fault," Damien said, "but it only makes me more determined to have this conversation with you."

Allie straightened her shoulders. "I'm ready."

Damien turned to me. "Olivia?"

Oh, boy. I hadn't expected to be the interrogator. I had simply planned to stand by and be moral support for Damien. I drew in a deep breath and forced myself to make eye contact with Allie. "How much do you know about Sarah Alton's murder?" I asked.

Allie's mouth tightened. "This isn't about Kelly, then." When Damien and I both shook our heads, Allie continued, "All I know is that the police think she was dumped behind the dumpster—oof, sorry, that was an unintentional pun—and that she crawled to the stage door that opens onto the alley before she died. I also know she had an autographed CD from me. I had signed it to her earlier in the night."

"Do you know about the blood?" Damien asked.

Allie shook her head, and if she was lying, then she was doing a good job of it. She looked genuinely confused. "Blood?"

"More like the lack of it," I said. "The body didn't have much in it, and the police didn't find any behind the dumpster or at the stage door. They think they didn't find any because she was killed elsewhere, but we know it's probably because she was drained by a vampire."

Allie's mouth dropped open, and she stammered as she said, "I didn't know. Truly. I didn't kill her. I have donors in every city."

Damien wrinkled his nose. "Donors?"

"Yeah. They're fans who think it's cool they get to donate their blood to me."

"They know what you are?" I asked incredulously.

"Of course. You'd be surprised how willing people are to give me their blood."

"Not that surprised," I said honestly. "Vampire fantasies are alive and well. I think what surprises me is that you're willing to tell people what you are, and that they believe you."

Allie walked to one of the chairs and sat down. "It's not easy. Confide in the wrong person, and they either tell everyone you're nuts or, worse, they believe you but think you're a creature of hell and need to be destroyed. Jon has helped me come up with a good screening system over the years."

"Who's your donor here in Nightmare?" I asked.

Allie shook her head. "I don't have one. I did, but they moved away."

I sat down in the other chair. "No problem. While you're stuck here in Nightmare, you can mesmerize a tourist, like Mori does. None of the locals get suspicious, and the tourist simply wakes up the next morning with two small, unexplained puncture marks on their neck."

Allie dropped her head, and I could see the way her face flushed. "I can't do that. I have to have donors because I can't mesmerize."

CHAPTER TWENTY-ONE

I stared at Allie. "But you're a vampire," I said in disbelief.

Allie raised her head and looked at me sadly. "Yes, and apparently, it's incredibly rare for a vampire not to be able to mesmerize. Lucky me," she added sarcastically.

I tried to think of some way to console Allie, and all I could come up with was, "Theo doesn't have his fangs anymore, so he has a tough time, too."

"I met him last year. He seemed nice, and I had hoped we could hang out some on this visit to Nightmare." Allie shrugged. "But he wants nothing to do with me."

Great. I've just gone and made her feel worse.

"It's not your fault," I said. "Theo thought a vampire slayer was after you, so he wanted to stay somewhere safer." I had been trying to console Allie, and I just kept digging the hole deeper. Mentioning Theo's sleeping situation only highlighted the fact we had ruled out a vampire slayer, yet Theo was still staying in the mine. He probably trusted Allie and Jon no more than Mori did.

"I'm sorry you have such a big setback to drinking blood," Damien said, and I was surprised to hear what sounded like actual sympathy in his voice. "I can see why Jon is so overly protective of you. I'm sure it's hard coordinating willing donors when you're touring, and it must be frightening to have so many people know you're a vampire."

Allie nodded. "All it would take is for one of them to turn on me. Jon drives me absolutely nuts, but I couldn't do this without him."

"Why can't you just feed from him?" I asked suddenly. The comment I had overheard Jon making to Damien about Allie not being able to feed properly was making a lot more sense, but I didn't see why she couldn't simply get a new donor or two while she was stuck in Nightmare, starting with the person closest to her.

"I have. Twice this week already, but I can't take too much."

I bit my lip as I held a hasty internal debate. *I could do it,* I thought. *I could volunteer to be a donor.* I glanced at Damien. *So could he.*

Damien seemed to know what was running through my mind. He glanced at me with a slight frown before he gave Allie the same look. "You also could have asked Mori to do the mesmerizing for you," he pointed out.

"I didn't want anyone to know. It's kind of embarrassing. Plus, everyone here is already being so helpful, and the thought of asking for donors or help feeding seemed like too much. I was hoping this murder would be resolved quickly, and I could get back on the road." Allie lifted a hand, her fingers grazing her cheeks. "It's been four days, and I'm already showing signs of blood starvation."

"We'll come up with something," Damien said. Again, I could hear the sympathy. Damien had been so angry when Justine and I brought Allie and Jon to the Sanctuary, yet he was suddenly offering to be helpful. I wondered if it was because Allie had admitted she couldn't mesmerize. Even as a vampire, she was still an outsider, still different than every other vampire. Damien was an outsider, too, so maybe that was where the sympathy was stemming from.

"In the meantime," he continued, "tonight's meeting is starting soon. You two had better get to the dining room."

"And Jon?" Allie asked hesitantly.

"He'd better get there, too, if he wants to work tonight and earn some money." There was no need for Damien to add that Jon would be wise not to try starting another fight.

"I'll talk to him. Thank you. Both of you." Allie left in a hurry, like she was worried Damien might change his mind if she lingered.

I looked at Damien questioningly. "Are we going to set up a donor program for her?"

"I'm going to consider it. You need to get to the meeting, too."

Like Allie, I hustled out of Damien's office. Despite his sympathy for Allie's plight, his mood seemed to be darkening by the moment.

I walked to the dining room and settled in at my usual table. When I heard a *click-clack* behind me, I recognized the sound of Felipe's claws against the stone floor and knew Mori had arrived. Felipe hopped up onto the bench to my left while Mori gracefully slid into a spot on my right, her long purple gown not hindering her in the slightest.

"I understand I missed some drama earlier," Mori said in greeting.

I quickly filled her in on Jon's attack on Damien. Briefly, I considered not sharing Allie's news, but in the hope Mori might have some insight, I told her in a whisper that Allie couldn't mesmerize.

"Poor girl," Mori said. She, too, sounded sympathetic. "That's a hard life for a vampire. It means she either has to chase down her prey like a monster or talk someone into giving up their blood willingly."

"Allie says it's the latter."

"And yet there have been two murders on her two visits

to Nightmare. I wonder if the coroner checked to see if Kelly's body was missing a substantial amount of blood."

"You think Allie might have killed Kelly to drink from her?" I whispered.

"And framed it to look like the work of a slayer."

We both fell silent, and I was relieved when Justine stepped up to the podium and started the family meeting. I smiled to myself when she announced I would be stationed in the lagoon vignette. I always had fun donning a pirate costume and spending my evening with Theo and Seraphina.

Fridays were one of the busiest nights at the Sanctuary, so there was a steady stream of guests treading the low catwalk in the lagoon vignette. I was able to shut out all my doubts and worries for a while as I concentrated on scaring every single person as much as possible. After I made one burly man shriek, Theo grinned and gave me a high five.

Just a few minutes after midnight, the overhead lights blared to life, which meant the final guest of the evening had exited the haunt, and our job was done. I took off my tricorn hat and ran my fingernails across my scalp. I was beginning to consider growing my hair out so I could ditch the hat. My shoulder-length hair looked far too modern, so every time I played a pirate, I had to stuff it under the hat, which got hot and itchy after a while.

It had been an enjoyable night, but I was worn out, and I trudged to the dressing room to change back into my jeans and Sanctuary T-shirt. I grabbed my purse and was heading down the hall, calling good night to the others I passed, when Damien appeared in front of me. "Good night!" I said. Even I was surprised at just how cheerfully I had greeted him, but a fun night and knowing I'd be in bed soon had put me in a better mood.

"Not yet," he answered.

I huffed out a breath. "What now?"

"I want you to practice controlling your abilities."

"Again? Damien, I'm exhausted! The only thing I need to practice right now is falling into bed." I was whining, and I didn't even care.

Damien shook his head. "Come on." He turned on his heel, and I followed him to his office. As soon as we were inside with the door shut, he said, "I want you to concentrate, again, on getting information out of Allie. What she told us tonight about not being able to mesmerize is huge, and it's clearly not information she wants people to know. I think your focus last night on getting her to open up has finally paid off."

"Or maybe she just told us because she wanted to, and magic wasn't involved at all," I snapped.

"Please, Olivia. If it did work, then it could work again. I need you to focus, and I need you to believe it's possible."

I wasn't going to get out of this, so I sat down and propped my elbows on my knees. "Well… I'd like to get a look inside the room Allie and Jon are staying in. Jon barely opened the door earlier, so we couldn't get a peek inside. Then, when we told Allie we needed to talk to her, she suggested we come here, to your office. I want to know why we weren't invited in. Maybe they're just messy and don't want us to see what slobs they are, or maybe they're hiding something."

"Like another dead body?" Damien asked.

"Hopefully, it's nothing as bad as that."

"Focus on it, Olivia. Picture opening their door and walking inside, and feel how much you want that."

I dropped my head until my forehead was resting on my hands, and I shut my eyes so I could visualize exactly what Damien had told me to.

The next thing I knew, Damien's hand was on my shoulder, shaking me. I sat up quickly. "What?"

"You fell asleep."

"In my defense, I told you I was exhausted," I said groggily. "And I really was doing what you told me to before I drifted off."

"I know."

The self-satisfaction in Damien's voice made me wary. "Oh, no. Was I talking in my sleep?"

Damien shook his head, smiled, and pointed to the far corner. I looked up to see McCrory standing there, one leg of his ghostly form merging into the bookcase next to him.

"Sorry to wake you, Miss Olivia," McCrory said, "but I thought you and Mr. Shackleford would want to know that we overheard Allie and her manager saying they're heading to Under the Undertaker's. The lady says she's desperate to go out and have a little fun."

"Does the bar serve blood?" I asked.

"That I don't know, but since they serve Nightmare's supernatural residents, I think it's likely they keep some on hand for the vampires."

I glanced at Damien. "This is good. It's a straightforward way for her to feed."

Damien chuckled. "You're missing the obvious." When I just stared at him blankly, he said, "They're going to be out for a while, which means we can take a look around their room."

"Coincidence," I muttered.

"Maybe. Maybe not. Either way, let's go take a look."

McCrory walked with us to the basement, telling us that Malcolm, Gunnar, and Zach had all gone to Under the Undertaker's, too, to keep an eye on Allie and Jon. Tanner was waiting for us outside the vampire guest room.

Damien produced a set of keys, and soon, he was swinging the door open. He turned on the light as he went inside, and I followed. There was a polished black coffin in one corner and a twin mattress lying on the floor nearby. As it turned out, Allie and Jon were not slobs at all. The room was immaculate, with clothing neatly stacked in open suitcases on a small table, Allie's guitar in a stand, and toiletries in a perfect line on top of an antique dresser.

There was also a large red cooler sitting on the floor. Curious, I walked over to it and lifted the lid. Inside were neat stacks of empty plastic containers. *If containers like that were in my fridge, they would be full of takeout ramen,* I thought.

But this was Allie's cooler, not my fridge, and I expected the containers were for storing blood. Each container had a handwritten label on the lid, and I peered at one of them. *Eleanor, Clifton, AZ, August 7.*

My thoughts went back to the night I had seen Allie drinking from a Styrofoam cup during our shared break, and Tanner's comment about her drinking blood from a cup "like it was whiskey."

"Allie doesn't feed directly from her victims," I said. "Their blood is collected into containers. That's why there was no blood at the scene of the first murder."

CHAPTER TWENTY-TWO

"This doesn't prove Allie killed Sarah," Damien cautioned me.

I straightened up and turned to him. "You're right. At the same time, it doesn't look good." I swept my arm around the room. "Look how meticulous this room is. And there's not a drop of blood in that cooler. Allie is bleeding her victims with precision, and it looks as though she thoroughly cleans up after herself."

"Now we know why they didn't want us in here, at least. Allie and Jon would have known this"—Damien gestured toward the cooler—"storage system would raise questions."

"What should we do? Call the police?"

"And tell them what, Olivia? That we're harboring a vampire, and that she stores the blood of her donors in neat little plastic containers?" Damien shook his head. "No, we go talk to her again."

"Want me to come along?" McCrory asked.

"Yeah, and I'd like to bring Mori and Theo, too, if they haven't left yet. Olivia, can you please look for them in the dining room?"

As I was walking out of the guest room, I heard McCrory let out a whoop. "Just like we used to do things! Come on, Tanner, we're rustlin' up a posse!"

Mori was in the dining room, talking to Seraphina and the witches, but they told me Theo had already headed back to the mine. When I filled them in on what was going on, Mori quickly agreed to join me.

As we turned to leave, Madge's hand darted out and caught mine. "It makes sense now!" she cried. "The manager wasn't asking about hypnosis for some sinister purpose. He must be looking for an alternative to mesmerizing. Life would be so much easier for Allie if she had that ability."

"It does make sense," I agreed. "The donor system has been working for them, until now, so Jon is looking for alternatives."

Madge sighed. "Thank goodness. I was imagining the worst."

"If Allie turns out to be innocent, then maybe you three can teach her hypnosis, after all."

"Yes, we would be glad to. I hope she is innocent."

"Me, too," I said, even though I very much doubted she was.

By the time Mori and I reached the entryway, Damien had already retrieved the wooden box that contained Tanner and McCrory's six-shooters. The ghosts were tied to the guns they had used to kill each other in the middle of High Noon Boulevard, so they could only go with us to Under the Undertaker's if the guns went, too.

Damien drove. I volunteered to cram into the back seat of his Corvette so Mori could sit up front. I was taller than her, but I also wasn't dressed in a floor-length gown. Not only was I wedged in the back seat, but so were Tanner and McCrory. Of course, as ghosts, they didn't mind the tight squeeze. They were sitting on either side of me, and we were so close their arms kept disappearing into my own. It didn't hurt, but it was a little unsettling to watch, and it felt icy. By the time we had made the short drive, I was shivering, partly from the cold and partly from the creepy sensation of having ghosts passing through me.

Since cars weren't allowed to drive on High Noon Boulevard and there was no parking in the alley where Under the Undertaker's was, we parked as close as we could and walked over. I was carrying the worn wooden lockbox with the six-shooters as Tanner and McCrory floated on either side of me.

Just before we ducked into the alley, I saw a couple freeze as they crossed the road, staring at us. They had spotted Tanner and McCrory, whose semi-transparent forms and the glow they emitted were a dead giveaway that they were ghosts.

The man shouted, "Dudes, we loved the shootout! Awesome show!" He raised his arms and gave the ghosts two thumbs up, then burped loudly. He and his companion went on their way, laughing and swaying slightly.

Good thing they're too drunk to tell the ghosts from the reenactors, I thought. McCrory was grinning proudly, and Tanner wasn't floating so much as he was swaggering as he drifted into the alley.

Damien approached the door to the bar and knocked. The small window in the door slid open, and a pair of eyes peered out. I couldn't make out the words between Damien and the fairy, but the conversation sounded strained on both sides. Eventually, the window slid shut with a metallic snap, and a moment later, the door creaked open. Damien waved all of us through, and I followed Mori inside and down the spiral staircase that led to the basement. In that moment, I was more worried about Mori tripping on the hem of her gown than I was about the confrontation we were about to have, but I should have known she would get down the stairs as gracefully as she did everything else.

Unfortunately, I was so focused on Mori that I wasn't

thinking about myself. I stumbled halfway down, and Damien, who was behind me, had to reach out and steady me with a hand on my arm. "Thanks," I muttered. After that, I focused on getting myself safely down the stairs and stopped worrying about anyone else.

Under the Undertaker's was a dark, elegant bar, with long curtains hanging between the low tables to create alcoves filled with the glow of candles.

We spotted Malcolm, Gunnar, and Zach first. For one thing, Gunnar was impossible to miss because of his massive size. For another, the three of them stood out from the crowd because they were blatantly staring at the table across from them, where Allie and Jon sat huddled together.

Damien and I headed straight for Allie and Jon, while Mori and the ghosts trailed behind us. Even in the dim lighting, I could see Allie was drinking what appeared to be blood out of a wine glass. My stomach lurched, and I focused my gaze on Allie's face, instead.

Allie simply looked around at all of us nervously, while Jon stood up so abruptly his stool went toppling backward. "Are you going to harass her here, too?" At least, this time, he wasn't shouting, but he was loud enough that everyone seated nearby turned to stare. "We came here to get away from you!"

Damien ignored Jon. Instead, he said to Allie, "Let's talk about your donors."

"What about them?"

"We found the cooler in your room," I said.

Jon lunged toward me, but Damien threw out his arm, his hand pressed against Jon's chest. Jon backed away while he hissed, "And now you're invading her privacy?"

"If I have a murderer staying under my roof and endangering my employees, then I have a right to know," Damien said. He dropped his arm, and when I looked at him, I could see the faint green glow in his eyes. It wasn't a good sign. Malcolm, Zach, and Gunnar all rose and joined our group, clearly ready to provide backup, if it was necessary.

Quickly, I said, "Allie, do you collect the blood from all your donors in containers, or do you drink from some of them directly?"

Allie looked uncomfortable, her eyes flicking between Damien, Jon, and me.

"You don't have to answer her questions," Jon said. "You don't owe these people anything."

"We owe them a lot," Allie said firmly. "They took a big risk bringing us to the Sanctuary."

"You didn't kill anyone, and you don't need to answer their questions," Jon insisted.

"You're right. I don't need to. I want to." Allie looked at me, the resolution clear in her expression.

"How does the whole process work?" I asked.

"We know who my biggest fans are. They're the ones who have signed up for my newsletter, email me with offers to put up flyers before shows, buy every single piece of merchandise I put out… You know how it goes."

I didn't, since I wasn't a musician, but I nodded sagely so Allie would go on.

"Jon reaches out to those fans, feels out their willingness to really, truly do anything for me, then signs them up as donors. I have one in each town we visit."

"Then you cut them open and fill up your cooler?" Damien asked.

Allie shook her head. "I don't collect or drink from my donors. I'm not even present when their blood is collected. I don't know their names, and if I meet them at a show, they know they're not supposed to mention they're a donor. We thought involving me as little as possible was safest. It's a risky enough setup as it is."

"If you're not the one collecting the blood," I began, but there was no point finishing my question. Every head turned toward Jon, who made a growling noise in his throat.

"Jon arranges all of it." Allie's voice was barely above a whisper.

I looked at Jon. "What happened here in Nightmare last year? Did you get a little carried away with Sarah's donation?"

Jon said nothing, but Allie said tensely, "My donor here moved away. That's what Jon said. That girl who was murdered, it didn't have anything to do with us." When Jon continued to stare down into his cocktail, sitting so still he might have been carved from stone, Allie reached a hand toward him. "Jon, please tell me you didn't kill Sarah."

"It's not a perfect science," he said, so low we all had to lean down to hear him. "Some donors can fill up three containers without even passing out. This one, though, she couldn't handle it. I managed to stop the bleeding, but I had taken too much. She didn't survive."

CHAPTER TWENTY-THREE

Allie pulled her hand back and stared at Jon. She had a look on her face that could only be described as anguish, though she didn't really seem surprised.

She knew, I thought. *She already knew, deep down, but she didn't want to admit it to herself.*

"I'm sorry," Jon said. To his credit, he sounded like he meant it.

"You know a murder like that could have exposed the vampires who live here in Nightmare, don't you?" Mori asked. I had only seen her angry once before, and it was scary. She wasn't yelling, but she was scowling at Jon in a way that made her look more like a monster than a beautiful woman. Plus, I could feel the emotion radiating off her. "There are some people in this town who know what we are, and they have agreed to keep our secret. But if any of them had suspected for a moment Sarah's death was due to one of us..." Mori's words trailed off into a guttural noise. I wasn't sure if she was imagining what could have happened, or imagining what she wanted to happen to Jon in that moment.

Jon shrank back in his chair. "It really was an accident."

"What do we do now?" I asked Damien.

"A human was murdered by a human. None of us at

the Sanctuary was involved in the woman's death. That means we call the police."

Allie bolted from her chair, and she stretched one arm in front of Jon protectively. "No, please! Don't take him away from me! I can't survive without him. How else will I get blood?"

"What did you do before you found Jon?" Mori snapped.

Allie's lip trembled, and she shook her head resolutely. "I refuse to talk about that period of my life. Luckily for me, I found Jon only two years after I turned."

"He's not that old, so that means you're a young vampire," Mori continued. "I'm sure you've realized that Jon is going to grow old and die. There will come a day when you have to survive without him. It might as well be today."

"I'm going to make him a vampire someday, when I'm confident I can do it right," Allie said. "He'll be able to mesmerize for both of us."

Mori looked like she wanted to retort, but Damien spoke first. "How many others have there been?" he asked Jon.

There was no hesitation as Jon answered, "She's the only one." He looked right into Damien's eyes as he said it, and I got the feeling he was being honest.

I was surprised when Malcolm spoke up. "Most of us at the Sanctuary have regrettable actions in our past," he said gently. "Your father, Damien, knew every one of mine, yet he still welcomed me. Jon might not be supernatural, but he works hard to keep a supernatural creature alive. Sometimes, in that line of work, accidents happen."

I stared at Malcolm, partly because I hadn't expected him to stick up for Jon, but mostly because I was wondering what "regrettable" things he had done. Had Malcolm killed someone, too? I didn't even know what he was. Malcolm had never displayed any supernatural talent, like Justine and her telekinesis or the witches and their spells, but he wasn't a vampire, a fairy, a banshee, or any of the other creatures who lived at the Sanctuary.

What is Malcolm, and how dark is his past?

Before I could linger on the question, Damien said, "Of course you're bringing my father into this. The old 'What would Baxter do?' approach." Damien looked angry for a moment, then his expression turned thoughtful. "He would have weighed the intent versus the outcome, and he would have wanted to see signs of true regret."

"Yes," Malcolm agreed.

"I do regret it," Jon said in rapid-fire delivery. There was an edge of hysteria in his voice and glance. "Of course I regret it. I never wanted to kill anyone, especially not someone as sweet and kind as Sarah. But she just collapsed in the van, and I tried to help her, but there was no pulse, no matter how hard I tried. And then I panicked, because there was a dead woman in our van, and it was my fault. So when I pulled into the alley to load up after the show, I dragged her body over behind the dumpster. It was only when the police called us that I found out she had still been alive." Jon looked pleadingly at Allie. "If the police had searched our van, they would have found the containers of blood and your bed. There would have been so many questions, questions we could never answer honestly."

No wonder Jon had seemed so timid when I first met him. Not only was he obsessed with keeping Allie safe and satiated, but he was also desperate to hide the fact he had killed someone.

"If this was truly an accident," Damien said slowly, "then you go free. And we will know the truth soon, because we're going to have the witches put a spell on you to make you tell the truth."

Madge had been against working such magic before,

but I expected this was a rare case in which a truth-telling spell was, in fact, the right course of action. If we were going to let Jon go free instead of hauling him to the police, then we needed to know he was being absolutely honest about Sarah's death being an accident.

I suddenly felt a strange sensation across my upper back and shoulders. My skin was crawling. I didn't like being in this morally gray area, even though I understood that supernatural matters sometimes had to be separated from human matters. My life had been a mess by the time I left Nashville, but at least I hadn't been part of an informal, magical jury.

Every single patron at Under the Undertaker's stared at us while we marched out of the bar. Damien walked closely behind Jon, but all the fight seemed to have gone out of him. If he had been hiding such a massive secret, then it was no wonder he had gotten so angry when Damien and I had begun asking questions. Jon hadn't been trying to protect Allie at all. He had been trying to protect himself.

Once we were outside in the alley, Damien instructed Mori and Zach to join him in walking Allie and Jon back to the Sanctuary. All five of them looked like ordinary humans, so any tourists who happened to spot them wouldn't think a thing of it. Gunnar said he would take the back roads, where he was unlikely to be spotted, and I offered to go with him.

Damien shook his head and reached toward me, his car keys dangling from his hand. "Olivia, you take my car so I can walk with the others. Tanner and McCrory will ride with you. Hurry back and let the witches know to meet us in the dining room."

The whole evening was so surreal I didn't even feel nervous about driving Damien's car. Soon, we were back at the Sanctuary. I carried the six-shooter box inside and headed directly up the stairs, Tanner and McCrory floating in my wake. The witches were in their apartment, and when Madge answered my knock, I saw Maida and Morgan behind her.

"We felt you coming," Maida said.

"And we're ready to help," Morgan added.

"What do you need?" Madge put her hands on my shoulders and looked at me intently. "You've had a shock."

"I'll explain in the dining room," I said, already turning to head in that direction.

We found a group of people at one of the tables in the dining room, engrossed in a card game. "McCrory, tell them they'll need to clear out," I said.

I sat down with the witches at a table and hastily filled them in while McCrory escorted the card players out of the room. "Madge," I concluded, "I know you said truth-telling spells weren't moral, but I'm hoping you'll make an exception."

All three witches nodded. "It's not proper to take away someone's right to lie," Maida said. "Magic should never impede free will."

"But if it's submit to the spell or go to jail, then the choice is clear," Morgan finished.

"They're right," Madge assured me. "If Jon submits to the spell willingly, it can clear him of any malicious intent. Sadly, it doesn't change the fact he killed someone."

My mouth twitched, and Madge caught my hand. "This is new to you, and you don't like it."

"I'm used to criminals going to jail."

"We're not bad," Maida said frankly. "We simply have our own system of justice that exists outside the laws by which you've always governed your life."

I gave her a small smile. "I just hope Jon doesn't literally get away with murder."

Gunnar had come in while we were talking, but he was

pacing a short distance away. When the others arrived, we all gathered around Damien.

"Ladies, where would you like to do this?" Damien asked the witches.

Morgan said, "In private."

"Preferably," Madge interjected.

Morgan continued, "Sometimes, a truth-telling spell can bring other secrets to light. Personal secrets that don't need to be known."

Jon didn't protest as the witches escorted him to the dressing room. As we waited for them to work their magic, Allie sat down next to me. "Speaking of secrets," she began, "I assume you found that note in the locker room."

"I did."

"I wrote it, but I wanted you to think Jon had."

I peered at Allie. "I did think Jon had written it. It only made you look more guilty of killing Sarah, so why would you do something like that?"

Allie sighed. "I didn't want to believe Jon had killed that girl, but I suspected it. I had fresh blood in the cooler the night after a fan of mine was killed, and then, shortly before we arrived here on Monday, Jon told me my donor had moved. It seemed like too much to be a coincidence." Allie sighed again and rubbed her hands over her face. "I thought you might stop looking into her death if you were convinced I had done it. Even if you hated me for it, at least Jon wouldn't get blamed."

I shook my head, surprised. "Even if I thought you were guilty—which I did—I would have still wanted to know the details. All that note did was convince me to keep digging."

"So I see. I underestimated your dedication to finding the truth."

After that, Allie fell silent. None of us had anything to say, and we all sat there anxiously, waiting for the witches and Jon to return. It was so quiet in the dining room I could hear the ticking of the clock on the wall, which told me they were only gone for fifteen minutes. In that short span, I had probably glanced up at the clock fifty times. Finally, the witches filed back in, with Jon behind them.

"He's telling the truth," Morgan announced. "He did not mean to kill the woman, and he truly tried to save her."

"What about Kelly Lowry's murder?" Damien asked.

"He is innocent on that matter," Madge said. "We do not know who killed her, or why, but it was not this man."

CHAPTER TWENTY-FOUR

I heard Allie breathe out a sigh next to me. "Oh, thank goodness." When I glanced at her, her eyes were closed, and her hands were clamped tightly together. She had been more worried about Jon's culpability than I had realized.

"Now we need to find the truth about Kelly's death," Damien said.

Allie's head snapped up as she opened her eyes. "It wasn't me! The witches can do the same spell on me, and they'll see I'm telling the truth!"

"Supernatural creatures aren't as susceptible to our magic," Morgan said.

Maida twirled one of her long braids in her fingers. "It might not work on you."

"I think we're going to have to take Allie's word for it," I said to Damien. "Now that we know the first death was accidental, it's looking even more likely that neither Allie nor Jon were involved in Kelly's murder."

Damien stared at me for a long time before he nodded curtly. "Get some rest. All of you. And thank you for your help tonight."

I went home that night exhausted and conflicted. Sarah Alton's death had been solved, and before I left the Sanctuary that night, Madge had promised me ominously that there would be consequences for Jon, even if it wasn't jail time.

I also went home alone. Mori was satisfied with the witches' report. She had been right to be wary of Jon, but knowing the truth, at least, made her realize she could safely sleep at the Sanctuary.

Falling asleep was easy for me, but I was disappointed when I awoke and saw the room was still dark. I had expected to get a solid night's sleep after all the events and revelations of the day. I stretched, turned on the nightstand lamp, and climbed out of bed. It was only then I remembered I still had aluminum foil taped over my windows. When I ripped the first piece down, the bright daylight that poured into my apartment made me squint and turn away.

I checked the clock. It was two in the afternoon.

I had been too exhausted the night before to prep my coffee maker, so I wasted no time getting it set up and percolating. As I continued removing the aluminum foil from the windows, I reflected that my current situation might be the closest I ever came to knowing what it was like to be a vampire. Dead to the world during the day, and unable to gaze outside because the sunshine was so bright it was almost painful.

Yeah, I definitely preferred being human.

My eyes had adjusted to the light by the time the coffee was ready, so I sat at my kitchen table and thought back over everything that had happened in the past week while I sipped carefully from my steaming mug.

One death had been explained, but there was still Kelly's murder to figure out. It hadn't been a vampire slayer, and it seemed not to have been a vampire, either. No one supernatural or related to the Sanctuary had been involved, or so it seemed, but I still wanted to know who was responsible.

So, after three cups of coffee—because I desperately

needed the boost—I showered, dressed, and headed out for the saloon. My plan was to visit Frankie again, but this time, I wasn't going to leave without getting some solid answers from him.

Except, when I arrived, I saw Miguel and Tara sitting together at a table. Their heads were close together, and Tara's fingers were resting lightly on Miguel's arm. I immediately forgot all about Frankie and made a beeline for the two of them.

No wonder Lottie told Emmett her new place wouldn't need space for Miguel since he'd be moving on soon.

Tara and Miguel were so busy looking at each other they didn't seem to notice me until I loudly pulled a chair out from the table and sat down across from them.

"Oh. Olivia." Miguel sat up straight, his expression quickly sobering.

"Hi, Miguel. Don't worry. I'm not here to ask you more bizarre questions. In fact, I came here hoping to chat with Frankie."

"He'll be in the office," Tara said, jerking a thumb toward the back wall of the saloon.

"I know, but since you're here, I thought I'd stop and talk to you again, too." I smiled as politely as I could, but Tara scooted her chair back and crossed her arms. She didn't tell me to get lost, though, so I continued. "I want to know if there are any more details you can give me about Kelly stealing money from this place. I think it might help us find her killer. Do you know if she ever tried to take money again after she was caught? Who caught her in the first place?"

"Frankie caught her," Tara said. She shifted uncomfortably.

"I wonder how much she really took, compared to what she claimed she took," I mused. "Eloping is cheaper than a big wedding, but it can still be expensive."

"Eloping?" Miguel looked at me in disbelief.

"Of course," I said. "Kelly told both Tara and her hairdresser that she was saving every penny so you two could elope. If it was supposed to be a secret, Kelly wasn't doing a good job of keeping it."

Miguel shook his head firmly. "But we weren't planning to elope! She brought it up, but I told her I wanted to have a traditional wedding here when the time came, with all of our family and friends."

"Why would Kelly have lied about eloping with you?" I asked.

"I don't know."

I remembered Allie had said Kelly asked her questions about life on the road and her favorite small towns. It was possible Kelly had been hoarding the money so she could get out of Nightmare, and the elopement story was just a good excuse as to why she was saving up to leave town.

Or, maybe, Kelly hadn't been planning on going anywhere, and the money was for something else. I couldn't imagine what, though. There weren't a lot of places in Nightmare to drop loads of money, unless she was planning on buying real estate or opening a business.

As I was sitting there, pondering the maybes, another one occurred to me: maybe it wasn't about the stealing. Maybe Kelly had been killed because of love rather than money, and I could be looking at the killer right that very moment. Tara was staring at Miguel, and if she were a cartoon character, her eyes would have been little hearts.

"You really weren't planning to run away with her?" Tara sounded relieved.

"We weren't even seriously talking about marriage."

Tara put her fingers on Miguel's arm again, smiling dreamily. Just as quickly, though, she frowned. "Then why was Kelly always broke? Even if she was paying Frankie back, she still had to bum gas money off other servers, and she would never go out unless someone else was buying."

"Those are questions I'd like answers to, as well," I said.

Miguel's gaze shifted to somewhere behind me. He quickly moved so he was no longer in physical contact with Tara. "I have to go," he said as he raised a hand in a wave. "My mom wants me to help her look at apartments."

I glanced over my shoulder and saw Lottie walking toward us. I smiled awkwardly at her. "I heard you were downsizing. I hope you find a nice place."

"I've struggled ever since the divorce. I'm amazed I was able to hang onto the house for as long as I did."

I gave Lottie a sympathetic look. "I know what it's like to be divorced and broke. I traded a big house for a tiny apartment at a motel."

Miguel laughed. "Mom has been complaining about money for years, but lately she's had wads of cash. I keep joking that she must have become a drug dealer. She's been swimming in ones and fives."

Even though Miguel found his joke funny, Lottie clearly didn't. Her face clouded over, and she raised the manilla envelope she was holding. "We have a lot of work to do."

Judging by the look Lottie was giving me, that work was strictly between her and Miguel. I rose, said a quick good-bye, and moved toward an empty stool at the bar. Tara followed me.

I sat so I could keep an eye on Miguel and Lottie, who was sitting in the chair I had vacated.

"She's like that sometimes," Tara said. "Don't be mad."

"I'm not mad. I'm looking at the woman who killed Kelly Lowry."

CHAPTER TWENTY-FIVE

Tara stared at me in a stunned silence as I pulled my cell phone out of my purse, my eyes still locked on the back of Lottie's head. Of course she hadn't laughed when Miguel had mentioned her sudden influx of cash. Ones and fives? That was probably tip money. Either Kelly had continued stealing from the tip jar after she had been caught, or she had been forking over her own tip money to Lottie.

I knew Lottie had never approved of Kelly because she didn't think she was good enough for her son. It was more than that, though, since Lottie also believed Kelly had killed Sarah. Instead of going to the police with her suspicions, she had blackmailed Kelly.

And Kelly, who didn't want to lose her boyfriend, had started making payments, even though she hadn't killed anyone. Maybe she had no alibi during the time of Sarah's death, or she worried the police would jump on the chance to close the case, even if there wasn't concrete evidence against her.

"Tara, I need the number for the police station." I waved my flip-phone while still staring at Lottie. "I can't look it up." Tara immediately produced her own phone, and soon, she was reading the number off to me. I finally peeled my eyes away from Lottie so I could punch in the numbers. A bored-sounding woman answered my call, and

I asked for Officer Reyes. I kicked my heel anxiously against the bar as I waited for the transfer.

"Officer Reyes here," came the familiar voice.

"Officer, it's Olivia Kendrick," I said quickly, cupping my hand over my mouth so I didn't have to shout over the din of the saloon. "I think Lottie Fernandez killed Kelly. I think she was blackmailing Kelly because she believed Kelly had killed Sarah Alton."

There was a long silence, and I wanted to reach through the phone and nudge Officer Reyes. Finally, after an agonizingly long time, he said, "You're two for two, Olivia. If you think it's worth my time, I'll have a chat with her."

"She's at the saloon, right now. She's going to look at apartments with Miguel and Emmett Kline in a bit."

"And I assume you're keeping an eye on her?" Despite the gravity of the situation, I could hear the amusement in Reyes's tone.

"Please, just get here!"

"I'm on my way. Remember, though, you're just speculating. I'm not coming to arrest Lottie but to chat with her."

"I know. Thanks." I hung up the phone, feeling breathless and anxious. What if I was wrong?

Tara turned toward the bartender, and it sounded like she was far away as I heard her demand two beers. Soon, she took my hand and gently wrapped my fingers around an icy mug. "You need a drink," she said.

The coolness of the mug helped clear my head, but I didn't take a sip. I was too busy staring at Lottie. She had been showing Miguel what I assumed were listings for vacant apartments, and now she was sliding them back into the manilla envelope.

Just as Lottie and Miguel stood to go, Officer Reyes came through the saloon doors. He was obviously in a hurry, and the doors swung back and forth a few times in his wake. He paused with his hands on his hips as his gaze roamed around the saloon.

I bet McCrory looked just like that when he used to come in here hunting for outlaws.

Lottie froze when she saw Reyes, and a wide, forced smile slowly appeared on her face. I couldn't see what the two of them said to each other when Reyes walked over, but I could see the way her smile faltered.

And then I saw Lottie turn and glare at me, her face transforming from a false sweetness to outright loathing. She began to run toward me, even as Reyes reached out to stop her but missed her arm by just inches.

There was nowhere I could go, so I slid off my barstool and braced myself for whatever was coming. I wasn't sure if Lottie was going to attack me with her words or her hands.

Lottie stopped so close to me that I could feel the air from her heavy exhales. I wrinkled my nose and turned away, leaning back as far as I could. "This is your fault!" Lottie shouted. "Why did you have to go looking into something that wasn't your business, anyway?"

Reyes had caught up to Lottie by that time, and he put a hand on each of her shoulders and pulled her away from me. Lottie didn't give up, though. She struggled against him, seething. "She deserved to die after what she did to Sarah! After what she did to my boy! Sarah was never good enough for Miguel, but her death broke him!"

"So you *were* blackmailing Kelly," I said. I could hear the disbelief in my voice. Even though I had been nearly certain my hunch was right, there was still that part of me that thought there was no way Lottie could have done such a thing to her son's girlfriend. "Now that Kelly is dead, though, you aren't getting the extra cash anymore, which is why you're selling your house and downsizing."

"She was supposed to have the next payment that night," Lottie said. "And she had the audacity to refuse to pay me! Can you believe it? She said she was going to spend the money on a lawyer, instead, so if I accused her of killing Sarah, she would have someone to get her off the hook."

"Did you kill Kelly because she refused to pay you blackmail money?" Reyes asked. From the sound of it, he was as incredulous as me.

Lottie made a guttural noise and took another lunge at me, but Reyes held her tight. "She started calling me names. Mean names. There was a pool cue leaning against the wall, and I broke it I was so angry. I still don't know how it wound up in her chest. I was just so mad."

Miguel's voice broke as he said, "Mom..." My heart broke for him. When he had blamed himself for Kelly's death, saying she would still be alive if he hadn't brought the pool cue to the saloon, I had told him he was wrong, because the killer would have found some other weapon.

Instead, Miguel's instinct had been right. The killer had acted on impulse, and if the pool cue hadn't been in reach, Kelly might have survived the night. To make it even worse, the killer was his own mother. I suspected Kelly's dreams of leaving town had been about escaping Lottie's threats, right up until the moment she decided to fight back by hiring a lawyer instead of running away.

Reyes was putting Lottie in handcuffs even while she was still trying to close the small gap between us. He turned her around and steered her out of the saloon with Miguel trailing behind them, his head down.

Everyone in the saloon had fallen silent during Lottie's confession. The only sounds were from the country music playing quietly over the speakers and the hum of the ceiling fans. As Reyes and Lottie disappeared outside, I noticed several tourists appeared to be filming the whole thing.

I slowly turned, sat down on the barstool, and took a long gulp of my beer.

Tara and I spoke very little as we sat there. Every now and then, she would mutter, "I just can't believe it," and I would answer, "Me, neither."

Eventually, Tara plunked down her beer mug and said, "I have to get to the police station. Miguel is going to need me."

I told her I'd pay the tab and wished her luck. It was only after she left that I realized people were staring at me. Not wanting to wind up on some tourist's video myself, I put cash down on the bar and left.

I stopped in at the motel office before returning to my apartment. Mama hadn't heard the news yet, and her blue eyes seemed to grow five sizes in her face as I filled her in. When I was done, she just shook her head and said, "Mothers will do anything to protect their sons, but it sounds like Lottie let greed get in the way of love."

I leaned forward and rested my elbows on the Formica countertop. "That's what I don't get. It sounds like Lottie would have let her son marry a woman she believed to be a killer, as long as she kept getting cash. It's disgusting."

"That poor boy. He's lost two girlfriends in a year, and now, he's lost his mother, in a way."

"At least he got to grow up with a mother," I said. I lifted one hand to my necklace. "Damien never even knew his."

Mama looked thoughtful. "I'm not sure what's worse: never knowing your mother or finding out your mother is a murderer."

"I don't know." I pushed myself up off the counter. "Speaking of Damien, I should go tell him the news. He'll be relieved to know Allie and her manager aren't involved in any of this."

I desperately wanted to go upstairs to my apartment and fall into bed. I felt mentally drained after everything that had happened, and I told myself I could just call Damien rather than drive over to the Sanctuary. In the end, though, I decided it was news best delivered in person.

Allie wouldn't be awake until sundown, and I knew she would be happy to hear she and Jon would soon be cleared to start touring again. In the meantime, though, I went in search of Damien when I got to the Sanctuary so I could tell him the news. His office was locked, and there was no answer to my knocks. I decided to look for him in the haunt itself, and I was about to go through the door that led into it when I heard Zach call my name. I stopped and turned, and my face must have given me away, because he said, "They found the killer, I assume."

"And it's no one at all related to the Sanctuary or the supernatural community."

"Good. If you came here to tell Damien, I saw him heading toward the trail."

"Trail?"

"Behind the building. There's a trail that leads out to the old hospital cemetery."

I thanked Zach and went out the front door, choosing to walk around the outside of the building rather than trying to find my way to a back door. The sun was still above the distant mountains, and I squinted in the late-afternoon glare. There was a small open space behind the Sanctuary that was well tended, and I spotted a grill, a few picnic tables, and some lounge chairs. Beyond that, the land was wild, and there was only one clear path through the scrubby trees and underbrush.

I found Damien sitting on a stone bench just inside the

low iron fence surrounding the cemetery. The headstones were mostly small and uncarved, though there were a few statues of cherubs and weeping women scattered around. The bench Damien was on sat underneath a tree, so it was a nice shady spot for taking in the view.

"What are you doing out here?" I asked as I sat down next to Damien.

Damien turned to me with a smirk. "I do leave my office from time to time, you know."

"Do you know anyone buried here?" By the looks of it, Damien had been born at least a century after the cemetery was founded.

"A few Sanctuary old-timers who died before I left Nightmare are buried here. I used to play out here a lot as a kid. Growing up at the Sanctuary, it's hard to feel scared by a bunch of dead bodies."

"A dead body is the reason I'm here. I came to tell you Kelly's murderer has been arrested."

"And you're the one who figured it out." It was a statement, not a question.

"Well…" I thought about taking the humble route, but I soon found myself telling Damien every detail of my realization Lottie had been blackmailing Kelly, wrapping up my story with the confrontation in the saloon.

When I was finished, Damien laughed. "Your conjuring skills worked."

"My ability to think worked," I argued. Damien was ruining my gloating. "I used my brain, not magic."

"You did use your brain." Damien looked at me earnestly. "Me saying you accomplished this with the help of your conjuring skills doesn't diminish your intelligence. You're using the two things together to get extraordinary results. You haven't even been in this town for two months, and you've already solved four murders, including one that happened before you ever arrived in Nightmare."

I didn't have the energy to argue, and since Damien had kind of complimented me, I decided to let it go. Instead, I said, "Now Allie and Jon can get back on the road."

"Not yet. First, we have to decide how Jon will be punished for killing Sarah Alton."

CHAPTER TWENTY-SIX

Damien wouldn't let me listen in on the discussion about how to deal with Sarah's accidental death. I begged him on the entire walk from the cemetery back to the Sanctuary to let me be a part of it, but he refused, over and over. Finally, when we reached his office, Damien spun around abruptly and clamped his hands on my shoulders. He leaned his face close to mine, and I tilted back when I saw the spark of green in his eyes.

"You're still new to this world, Olivia. You shouldn't have to be burdened with matters like this. Not yet."

"What are you trying to protect me from?" I asked quietly.

Damien's fingers loosened, but his hands still rested on my shoulders. "Someone is dead, and we have to determine what happens now to the person who killed her. You have no idea what a painful responsibility that is. I barely slept last night, because I knew we would have to find a fitting punishment for Jon. I'm not going to pull you into that. After everything you went through before you got to Nightmare, I can't do that to you."

There was still a glow in Damien's eyes, but it seemed deep, nearly hidden under the pain in his gaze.

"What a terrible week you've had." I hadn't meant to

say it out loud. It was more like a thought that found an escape route through my mouth.

Damien's jaw clenched, and his eyes closed briefly. Instinctively, I lifted my arms, ready to reach out and pull Damien into a hug. Before I could, though, I heard footsteps in the hallway, followed by Zach's voice. "We're ready when you are, Damien."

I turned around, hastily stuffing my hands into the pockets of my shorts as I did so. I felt slightly embarrassed, like I had been caught doing something I shouldn't have been. Zach looked grim, and I wondered if he also felt the weight of having a man's fate in his hands. Damien didn't even look at me as he moved past me and left with Zach. I trailed after the two of them slowly, and I saw both Malcolm and the witches walking through the entryway. They were all heading for the dining room.

I knew I shouldn't feel left out. Damien was trying to protect me, and I could appreciate that, but I was also curious to know how it would all work. Were there supernatural laws? Was someone going to pull out a book and look up *Murder, accidental* in some kind of paranormal punishment encyclopedia?

There were still a couple of hours before work started, so I drove back to the motel. I tried to nap, but instead, I just lay on my side, staring at the wall as I pictured my friends sitting around a table in the Sanctuary's dining room.

Just when I thought I was getting used to living and working alongside supernatural creatures, I'd had a curveball thrown at me that left me feeling uncomfortable and out of sorts.

Maybe it's time for me to finish what I started, I thought. *I can put in my notice at work tonight and hit the road for San Diego tomorrow.* My brother had been furious when I had finally called to tell him I had never arrived at his house there because I had broken down in Nightmare. He said he had been ready to call the police since no one had heard from me.

But he hadn't called the police. I had disappeared, and my own brother hadn't cared enough to do something about it.

No, I wasn't leaving Nightmare. The friends I had made since being stranded in the quirky old mining town cared about me. They accepted me for who I was, and they looked after me. Even Damien, who could be the biggest jerk in the world, was trying to protect me. He cared more about me than my own brother.

"Oh, no," I moaned. I was in danger of not disliking Damien anymore.

I'm not saying I liked him, but I was definitely beginning to feel less resentful toward him. It wasn't just this supernatural justice thing Damien was shielding me from, either. Damien had watched over me when I was threatened during my first week in Nightmare. He had given me his mother's necklace, which had a powerful protection spell on it. And, this time, he was protecting me from the heartache of deciding someone's fate.

When I went back to the Sanctuary for work that night, I made a beeline for Damien's office. I didn't wait for him to invite me in, and I didn't ask if he had time to talk. I just shut the door behind me and sat down. Damien opened his mouth to say something, but I cut him off. "Are you doing okay?"

"I'm doing better, as a matter of fact. I'm pleased with the result of our council."

I swallowed nervously. "What's going to happen to Jon?"

"Sarah was a willing blood donor for Allie, and Jon tried to save her. Still, the fact remains she died while under his care. I think we came up with a fitting punishment. I'm going to talk the saloon into hosting an annual fundraiser in Sarah's name, with all proceeds going to the charity of her family's choice. The biggest donor for the next ten years will be Jon, albeit anonymously. Additionally, when Jon isn't on tour with Allie, he has to commit to at least five hours of volunteer work every week, and yes, we will be checking to make sure he's following through."

I laughed out of pure relief. "That's it? I was worried you were going to march him down to the gallows at the crossroads, or worse."

Damien shrugged. "In the supernatural community, setting someone on a better path is preferable to locking them up or, as you say, marching them to the gallows. Jon still has the potential to do some good in this world. We thought it best that he should pay for his mistake in a way that will be beneficial to others."

"I think it's a good plan. I hope I get to say goodbye to Allie before they hit the road."

"They'll be at the meeting tonight. We're going to tell everyone what happened, so they know Allie is innocent and Jon is being dealt with."

I leaned forward. "When I asked if you were okay, Damien, I didn't just mean about what happened this afternoon."

"I know," Damien answered quietly. "That mine… The photo of my mother… You were drawn to that place because you heard my father's voice coming from it. You—and I—were meant to go in there. Right now, that mine is only raising more questions, but I think it will help lead us to answers."

"I'm going to go home after work tonight and sleep harder than a vampire at noon. Then, tomorrow, I'd like to practice controlling my conjuring with you. If that's okay."

Damien looked surprised. I couldn't blame him. I was a little surprised myself. But he was right. That mine was a mystery in and of itself, but I was certain it would help us find Baxter. Maybe I had been drawn to it through some kind of magical connection. Whether it was a magic within me or from an outside source, I wasn't sure. Regardless, I knew I needed to pursue every possible way to help Baxter, even if it meant practicing a skill I didn't even believe I possessed.

"That would be great," Damien said, smiling faintly. "How about noon at your place? I'll bring lunch."

The family meeting that night was long, but I could almost feel the collective sigh of relief from everyone. Theo was sitting next to me, and afterward, he said, "No vampire slayer in sight, and those two had nothing to do with Kelly's murder. I've been sleeping in an old mine for nothing!"

"Does that mean you're moving back in?" I asked.

"I'll be in my own bed at dawn!"

There were several people waiting to talk to Allie and Jon when I walked toward the podium, where they were standing. When it was my turn, Allie hugged me tightly. "Thank you for clearing my name, Olivia. I'm so grateful to you. We're hitting the road tonight, and I'll be singing in Flagstaff tomorrow!"

"I hope the rest of your tour is great."

Jon and I said a brief, polite goodbye to each other. He would never be a fan of mine for uncovering the truth about Sarah, but he didn't seem to be holding too much of a grudge against me.

I was stationed at the front door that night, tearing tickets for the huge Saturday night crowds. The constant stream of people finally began to slow around eleven o'clock, and during a break between arriving guests, I looked up to see Zach gesturing to me.

I hurried over to the ticket window. "What's up?" I asked.

"Should I put you down for a side dish or beverages?"

I stared at Zach blankly. "What?"

"For the party."

"I have no idea what you're talking about."

Zach laughed and shook his head, his rust-red hair dancing over his shoulders. "Of course! This is going to be your first time with us! Next Friday is a Friday the Thirteenth, and we always have a party. After work, we grill out back and party under the stars. Seraphina sings for us, and if Malcolm drinks enough, he does some dance that was popular probably a hundred years ago. Everyone brings a side dish or drinks to share, so what can I put you down for?"

Zach was inviting me to a supernatural potluck. I grinned. "Macaroni and cheese. Thank you for including me."

"Of course," Zach said. "You're part of the family."

I bit my lip, willing myself not to start crying in front of the grumpiest guy in all of Nightmare. "Yeah," I said. "I am."

A NOTE FROM THE AUTHOR

Thank you for reading *Slaying at the Saloon*! I'm having so much fun in the world of Nightmare, Arizona, and I hope you are, too. Things are going to take a dramatic turn in book four, *Murder at the Motel*, so I hope you're ready for the roller coaster ride!

Before you dive into the next book, though, please consider leaving a review for this one. It means a lot, and it really helps other readers find my work. Thank you!

Eternally Yours,

Beth

P.S. You can keep up with my latest book news, get fun freebies, and more by signing up for my newsletter at BethDolgner.com!

FIND OUT WHAT'S NEXT FOR OLIVIA AND THE RESIDENTS OF NIGHTMARE, ARIZONA!

Murder at the Motel

NIGHTMARE, ARIZONA BOOK FOUR

PARANORMAL COZY MYSTERIES

Murder hits close to home for Olivia Kendrick when her annoying neighbor at Cowboy's Corral Motor Lodge turns up dead. Did one of the other guests hold a grudge against Leonard Evers?

Even while she's eyeing a few shady suspects, Olivia can't help but blame herself. Maybe she really is a conjuror, and maybe she accidentally killed her downstairs neighbor with magic.

With the help of her supernatural friends at Nightmare Sanctuary Haunted House, Olivia will spy on a plumber, get an eerie prediction from a psychic, and face veiled threats.

At the same time, Olivia's jerk boss, Damien Shackleford, learns a secret that will change the way he thinks of his family forever. Olivia must help Damien deal with the life-altering news, even while she tries to find the killer…

ACKNOWLEDGMENTS

As always, thank you to my eagle-eyed test readers: Sabrina, Lisa, Kristine, Mom, David, and Alex. Jena at BookMojo, thank you for your beautiful cover design, formatting, and marketing. I'm grateful to Lia at Your Best Book Editor and Trish at Blossoming Pages for helping me polish up the manuscript. And thank you to the last people to see a book before it debuts: my fabulous ARC readers!

ABOUT THE AUTHOR

Beth Dolgner writes paranormal fiction and nonfiction. Her interest in things that go bump in the night really took off on a trip to Savannah, Georgia, so it's fitting that her first series—Betty Boo, Ghost Hunter—takes place in that spooky city. Beth also writes paranormal nonfiction, including her first book, *Georgia Spirits and Specters*, which is a collection of Georgia ghost stories.

Beth and her husband, Ed, live in Tucson, Arizona. Their Victorian bungalow is possibly haunted, but it's not nearly as exciting as the ghostly activity at Eternal Rest Bed and Breakfast.

Beth also enjoys giving presentations on Victorian death and mourning traditions as well as Victorian Spiritualism. She has been a volunteer at an historic cemetery, a ghost tour guide, and a paranormal investigator. Beth likes to think of it all as research for her books.

Keep up with Beth and sign up for her newsletter at
BethDolgner.com

BOOKS BY BETH DOLGNER

The Nightmare, Arizona Series

Paranormal Cozy Series

Homicide at the Haunted House

Drowning at the Diner

Slaying at the Saloon

Murder at the Motel

Poisoning at the Party

Clawing at the Corral

The Eternal Rest Bed and Breakfast Series

Paranormal Cozy Mystery

Sweet Dreams

Late Checkout

Picture Perfect

Scenic Views

Breakfast Included

Groups Welcome

Quiet Nights

The Betty Boo, Ghost Hunter Series

Romantic Urban Fantasy

Ghost of a Threat

Ghost of a Whisper

Ghost of a Memory

Ghost of a Hope

Manifest

Young Adult Steampunk

A Talent for Death

Young Adult Urban Fantasy

Nonfiction

Georgia Spirits and Specters

Everyday Voodoo